Karma's a Bitch: The Sergio Pages Story

TO MY FRIEND DIANNE,
BE GOOD CAUSE KARMAS A
BITCH

Nikki Sinclair

DEDICATION

This book is dedicated to three my wonderful children, Jessica, Sergio Junior and Juan, and to my mom and dad. The lessons my parents taught me when I was growing up made me the man I am today. The lessons my children continue to teach me make me a better person.

Thank you. I will always love you all with all my heart.

Sergio Pages
September 2011
.

FOREWORD

This book tells the story of a surreal and nightmarish time in my life, when my faith in God and Jesus Christ was tested to its limits. I'm not proud of all the things I did during this time, but I did what I had to do to ensure the safety and security of my family.

I would be less than honest if I didn't include everything in the telling of this tale, even those things of which I'm less than proud. And, at my core, I'm an inherently honest man. So, here it is: Sergio Pages' story, warts and all.

I'm not perfect and have never professed to be so; I ask only that readers understand the desperate nature of the situation I was in. My financial security and mental health were taxed almost beyond endurance. I came close to throwing in the towel on more than one occasion.

I also ask readers to know that this story is a blend of fact and fiction, and that I have changed the names, actions and deeds of many of the characters in it. Any resemblance these characters might have to people, living or dead, is purely coincidental.

My interactions with the police officers who investigated the robbery of my store are based on fact and there were times when things did become heated. I was under a lot of pressure and, in those kinds of circumstances, it can be hard to truly see that someone is just trying to do their job. Despite any appearances to the contrary in this book, I have a huge amount of respect for the police and the job they do. I know it can be dangerous and dirty, and that they really do have to investigate all possible suspects when trying to solve a crime.

I have always supported the police, and will continue to do so, and I want to thank the Hillsborough County Sheriff's office. You guys rock. I also want to thank retired deputy Hugh Crawford. Hugh, your support and advice were always appreciated.

Even though I stumbled more than once and came close to losing my faith, the Lord continued to carry me and send me angels to comfort and guide me. I could not have done what I did and rebuilt my life and my business without the help of these angels who stood by me when everything and everyone else had deserted me. These loving and caring people were my silver lining; the dawn to my darkest night.

First and foremost is my loving son, Sergio Pages III, also known as Sergio Junior, who at this time is serving his country as an infantryman in the United States Army. Serge and his buddies are putting their lives on the line and taking the fight to the enemy in Afghanistan. I am so proud of you, son, and I pray God for your safe return to your family.

While Serge is away, my youngest son, Juan, has stepped into his shoes by helping me out at the store while also attending college. He says he wants to help me make Sergio's Jewelry even more successful so that Serge will have something good to come home to.

My nightmare started when Theresa, my wife, left me, taking my heart with her. She nearly took my sanity, too. During that time, a wonderful lady and new friend, Gail Nowland, showed me that angels can come out of nowhere and when you least expect them. I was a total mess at the time and her caring advice became some of the most important ammunition I had in my fight to keep myself from giving up completely.

Rebecca Teten is a sharp, articulate and intelligent woman who was there to shine a light for me in my blackest hours. She not only held my hand, but also helped me keep my sanity and stopped me from becoming a complete alcoholic. Her support touched my heart and I will go to my grave remembering her incredible generosity of spirit and the unwavering faith she had in me. She is an amazing woman.

When even my own mother and father deserted me, my Aunt Chicky and Uncle Frank stood by me. My cousin Danny and his wife Susan offered me $10,000 to help tide me over. I didn't accept it, not because I didn't appreciate their generosity, but because I couldn't risk losing their money. I believe they had more faith in me than I had in myself. And, I love them for it.

Jimmy Siccarello is a customer, former high-school classmate and hard-working Tampa realtor who loves Jesus Christ and isn't afraid to show it. Jimmy, the $500 you sent me during my hour of need was priceless beyond words. When I opened the envelope and read the note you'd sent with the check, I knew I could make it. You restored my faith when I felt I had nothing left to lose.

Last, but certainly not least, I want to thank my brother, John Pages and his beautiful, sweet wife, Lisa. John literally saved my life by persuading me to have gastric-bypass surgery, and he and Lisa were constant pillars of support through my toughest times. They were always there for me and even invited me to share Christmas with them when my own parents had turned their backs on me by inviting my ex-wife to spend the holiday with them rather than me. Lisa and John, your unwavering support and love sustained me and restored my faith in my family.

I could not have survived the ordeal God placed before me without the love and support of all these amazing people, as well as the countless customers and friends who called to check on me, sent cards of encouragement and love, and gave me moral support when I needed it most.

The final mention goes to the person without whom this book would never have been written: Nikki Sinclair. Our meeting was serendipitous, and she's a pain in the ass, but she knows how to craft a great yarn. And, she did more than just write this book, her loving and caring advice helped and encouraged me when I was struggling, and gave me something to live for.

Thank you all. May the good Lord bless you now and forever.

Sergio Pages
September 2011

Only the most bizarre and outlandish parts of this story are true...

I once read somewhere that everything that happens to you is your teacher, and that the secret is to learn to sit at the feet of your own life and be taught by it. If that's true, I must be a fucking PhD.

CHAPTER ONE

I'm gonna kill some motherfucker. That was my first thought. Son of a bitch, I'm fucking ruined. That was my second. I was numb, my brain unable to take in what my eyes were seeing. It was my worst nightmare multiplied by ten. No, by a thousand, and my head could only handle those two all-consuming thoughts. The sick feeling in the pit of my stomach started to work its way up to my throat. I thought I was going to throw up. I opened my mouth to breathe, but there was no air in the room. I might not be Vin Diesel, but I'm also not some sorry-ass wimp. I'm a Cuban/Puerto Rican from the Bronx. And some motherfucking bastard was gonna pay for this. Big time.

I was standing ankle deep in cold water with the remnants of my whole life flooding past me like life flashing before the eyes of a dying man. Around me was everything I'd worked so hard to build. And it looked like a war zone.

2

It had started out as a pretty ordinary Tuesday. Or as ordinary as any day had been since my wife had left. That was really when it had all started. When Theresa had left me. One minute, I was a happily married, successful guy who'd spent 25 years building a rocking jewelry business and raising three wonderful children with the most amazing woman in the world. I had everything I ever wanted. Great family, great wife, great business. Great life.

Then she dropped the bomb. I didn't even see it coming.

It was our 25th wedding anniversary and I'd booked us a dream vacation to Italy. It was particularly special because we'd never travelled outside of the country in our lives. Three days before the trip, she told me she was leaving. She said she still loved me, but that she didn't like me anymore. Then, she walked out and left me and the kids. Just like that. I mean, what's with that? Not even a conversation, just "I wanna show everyone I can make it on my own." What the fuck?

We'd been together for almost 30 years and I thought we were perfect for one another, soul mates, and that we'd grow old together. I'd taken care of her since we were 15 and I'd thought I was her rock. She was a hot babe, an awesome mom and a hardworking partner. We both had our faults, but I'd believed we were made for each other. I guess, in the end, she didn't feel the same way.

When she left, she took a piece of me with her, and I didn't begin to know how I was ever going to fill the hole she'd left behind. I couldn't even start to imagine my life without her.

I gave her half of everything. No fuss, no arguments, no lawyers. Just $50 for a paralegal to write up the divorce agreement and it was done. Just like that. She acted like it was no big deal. My heart was broken into so many pieces I was sure it would be impossible to ever put it back together again.

Bitch.

But, back to Tuesday morning.

I'd spent the night before at a Rough Riders' poker game. The roots of the Rough Riders can be traced back to Teddy Roosevelt's 1st Volunteer Cavalry, which fought in the Spanish American war and won the battle of San Juan Hill. They were also called the Rough Riders. Today's Rough Riders don't fight wars. They serve the community in other ways like handing out teddy bears to sick kids in hospitals. With a membership that's nearly 600 strong, the Rough Riders raise enough money to perform some heart-warming acts of charity. Like this grandma who was single-handedly trying to raise her two grandkids because their mother was in prison for drugs. The house they were living in was about to be condemned as uninhabitable and the grandkids taken into care by the state because the grandmother couldn't afford to feed the kids and fix up her home.

At first, we thought we'd just build her a new house, but a Rough Rider who's a lawyer pointed out that she'd never be able to afford the taxes on a new home. So, we took her house apart right down to the frame and then rebuilt it with new electrics and plumbing. We all pitched in what we could. I gave a $1,000 donation and encouraged all the other Rough Riders to do the same. Other people, like Csaba, the owner of Chuck's Plumbing, did work for free. When we were finished, we furnished the place and filled the pantry with food. It was awesome.

The Rough Riders are also one of the few parade crews in Tampa that's historically correct. And, we have poker games. We don't bet money or anything. It's just an excuse to hang out, have fun and get drunk with some good friends.

And, right then, drinking was just about the only thing that could fill the hole Theresa had left in my heart and kill the pain I felt every waking moment of every single day. Like a lot of people before me, I drank to forget.

That night, I'd gotten totally wasted. Again. I didn't even remember getting home, let alone whether I'd won or not. I was woken by sledgehammers pounding the inside of my skull. The bright January sunshine was streaming in through a crack in the blinds. It burned the backs of my eyeballs.

"Fuck." I rolled away from the light and buried my face in the pillow.

I felt sick. The inside of my head was spinning and something in my mouth tasted bad. I swallowed and realized it was my tongue. I had to stop drinking so much.

I fumbled on the nightstand for my Rolex Submariner and tried to see what time it was. The blue face of the watch was blurry and I had to squint to get it into focus. It was 8:10.

"Fuck." It seemed like the hangover had robbed me of every other word in my vocabulary. I was going to be late for work.

"What?" It was a woman's voice, dreamy and thick with sleep.

I didn't remember a woman from last night. I rolled over and pulled the sheet from her face. She was hot; tresses of long blond hair were splayed across the pillow. I wondered what her name was.

"I gotta get to work." It was the first thing that came into my aching head. I felt stupid the moment the words were out of my mouth.

There had been any number of women since Theresa had left me, but I'd always had some recollection of bringing them home, however drunk I'd been. But, I had no memory whatsoever of this chick.

"OK." She rolled over and picked up the clothes that were lying on the floor beside the bed. She swung a pair of long legs out of the bed and stretched like a cat before pulling the sheet around her and walking into the bathroom.

I grinned despite the thundering headache. I might not have been able to remember her name or anything else about her, but I could see she had a damn fine ass. I slumped back on my pillow, wishing I could remember something about last night. Sex with a woman that gorgeous had to have been amazing. Unless I'd been too drunk to be able to do anything with her. Fuck. I really had to stop drinking so much.

"You want a cup?" I motioned to the pot of coffee on the counter when she came into the kitchen. She looked every bit as good in her tight blue jeans and white shirt as she had wrapped in the bed sheet.

She shook her head as she rummaged in her purse, pulling out a set of car keys.

I cleared my throat. "Listen, uh, thanks for last night, OK?" I didn't really know what else to say.

"It's cool, Sergio." Her voice was rich and deep south. "Besides, hon, you were much too drunk to be able to drive yourself home. One of your Rough

Rider buddies said he'd get your truck back for you." A smile played with one side of her mouth. "He said that Rough Riders never leave a man down or his car behind."

That was just what my Rough Rider buddies would say and I knew my truck would already be parked outside my house.

And, then she left. Without another word and without telling me her name. I watched through the kitchen window as she walked to her car. God, she really was dripping hot. All legs. I sure as hell hoped I'd had hot sex with her the previous night even if I didn't remember. I also wished I hadn't made that stupid comment about work. If I'd been thinking straight, I could have stayed in bed with her for a while. Even if I did have the headache from hell, at least I would remember what we did. I cursed myself. Why hadn't I just stayed in bed with her? And, why the hell hadn't I asked her for her number or—

The noise of the telephone was very loud. I wondered if one of the boys had turned the ringer up to full volume again. I grabbed two more Tylenol and swallowed them with a gulp of coffee.

I picked up the phone. "Yeah? What?"

"Dad?" It was my eldest son, Sergio Junior. He's a good kid. Reliable. He runs the store when I'm not there. Today was his day to open up. "We've been robbed."

"What?" I got up fast, too fast. My chair crashed to the floor and I instantly regretted the sudden movement. And the noise. The room swam for a moment, the jackhammers in my head pounded harder, and my coffee slopped over the countertop and burned my hand.

"We've been robbed." Sergio Junior enunciated each word very carefully as if he was afraid of tripping over them.

"Fuck. How bad is it?"

"It's bad, Dad. Real bad."

I was expecting cops when I pulled into the parking lot of the strip mall at Gunn Highway and Casey Road where my store is. Lots of cops. There were none. Not a single one to be seen anywhere.

I parked my Hummer in front of the store and got out. The January sun was hot on my head and shoulders. At any other time, I would have enjoyed the warmth. Not today.

I pushed open the door, not quite sure what to expect. Sergio Junior had said it was bad, but how bad could it be if the place wasn't crawling with cops already?

The first thing I noticed was that the alarm didn't chime as it usually did when the door to the store opened. The second was the smell—the twin scents of smoke and ozone.

Then, I saw the inside of the store.

Sergio Junior hadn't been exaggerating. It was bad. Real bad. The beautiful jewelry store I'd started when I'd had nothing, and had worked so hard for more than 20 years to build, looked like it had been hit by a bomb. And a big one at that. Every display case was shattered and every piece of jewelry was gone. There was nothing left. Smashed and broken glass littered the floor.

Sergio Junior was standing at the far end of the store. He's a big, stocky guy with black hair and bronzed skin. Not many people would try to mess with him. Now he looked deflated. Shell-shocked. Half his usual size. And ashen. All the color was gone from his normally tanned face. He was standing beside Little Annie, who's been helping out at the store for more years than I can remember.

Middle-aged with mousy hair, Little Annie weighs in at 95 pounds and is so short she buys hookers' platform shoes just to be able to see over the counter. She looks like she'd be scared of her own shadow, but she's tough as shit. She's sharp, too, and has this glare that could kill a cockroach at 20 paces. She was at the store on her own one day when she caught this big, muscle-bound guy pulling a tray of rings out of a cabinet. She gave the guy one of her stares and told him to put the try down. The guy dropped the tray, turned tail and ran. She was laughing her ass off when she told me about it.

You need to be tough and sharp like that if you're in the jewelry business because it's a rough and dangerous trade. We're in an industry that puts us at extremely high risk of being robbed, which is why we keep guns everywhere. In fact, I pretty much always have a gun with me. I even keep a flashlight, gun and screwdriver hidden in the trunk of my car just in case I get attacked by someone and thrown in there. It's also no coincidence that jewelers are the number one purchasers of armored cars in America.

Since I've been in the jewelry business, my home's been invaded by a gang trying to steal from me and I've had people come into the store threatening me and trying to rip me off more times than I can remember. I need guns to protect myself, my family and my business. I'm not afraid to use them either.

Today, though, neither Sergio Junior nor Little Annie spoke. Neither of them could even look at me.

As soon as I saw the empty display cases, I thought about the safes. I crossed the store in two strides to the double swing doors that led into the back office. Broken glass crunched beneath my shoes.

If I thought the chaos in the store was bad, what greeted me when I pushed through the slatted doors into the back office was worse. A hundred times worse.

The place was flooded. Invoices and receipts were floating on several inches of scummy water. Chunks of concrete and metal from my three vaults were everywhere. Desks, chairs, computers, everything that could be moved, had been thrown into one corner of the room to make a space around the safes. The banners I usually put out on the roadside to attract customers had been nailed up over the doors and the two-way mirror, which let me see what was going on in the store when I was in the back office. I had a number of banners for different occasions, like Christmas and Valentine's Day, and when they weren't in use, I rolled them up and stored them in one corner of the office.

Then, there were the safes. I had three of them. They were high-security Diebold vaults, good ones, too. But, they'd been opened as easily as if they'd been sardine cans. There were scorch marks on the outsides. The thieves must have used some kind of cutting torch to open them. That would explain the smell, and the banners nailed to the door and the two-way mirror. They wouldn't have wanted any light to make its way outside and alert a passerby or, worse, the cops.

I squelched across to the vaults, my heart thundering. I was almost afraid to look. I was sure I'd find them stripped as bare as the display cases. Somewhere, something was dripping. A steady drip, drip, drip, drip. Like raindrops on plastic. I tried to ignore it as I looked into the first safe. I was careful not to touch anything. I'd watched enough episodes of CSI.

The safe was empty. Not even a single stud earring remained, just charred and burned chunks of concrete and splintered metal. The second safe was the same. I was fucked; the bastards had cleaned me out.

All I could think about were the customers who'd left jewelry with me for repair and the fact that I still owed Theresa $500,000 from the divorce settlement. I wasn't just fucked, I was fucking fucked.

I took a breath and then another before I was able to make myself slosh over to the third safe. My wet feet squelched inside my soaking shoes.

The third vault was different from the first two in that it had a small hidden compartment beneath the main body of the safe. Like the first two vaults, the main body of the third safe had been peeled open and ransacked. But, it looked like the thieves had missed the small hidden compartment. My heart skipped a beat.

I tried to open the hidden compartment, but my fingers were wet and slippery and shaking. I wiped them dry on my jeans and finally managed to key in the correct combination and open up the little door. I almost couldn't believe what I saw. Everything was still there. Thank God. I instantly wished I'd put all of the more valuable jewelry, and especially the diamonds, in this small safe when I'd locked up the night before. I banished the thought. This was no time for wishes and 'what ifs.' That wasn't the kind of person I was. I lived for the moment and made quick decisions. I made one right then: there was no way I was leaving this jewelry in the store one more minute. There were still no cops around, the store certainly wasn't secure and who knew whether the thieves would come back again.

I began lifting the jewelry out of the safe. There was nothing to put it in that wasn't soaking wet, so I gathered up as much as I could and carried it back out through the store to my truck. I knew Sergio Junior and Little Annie were staring at me, but neither of them said anything. They knew better than to ask questions.

I half walked and half ran to my truck, leaving a trail of wet footprints on the pavement. I opened the back of the Hummer and carefully placed the jewelry inside. Then, I went back into the store for more.

I was leaning into the truck and carefully laying down the fourth and final armful of jewelry from the safe when something blocked out the sunlight and made it difficult to see. I spun around.

A cop was standing behind me. He was young with a round face that hardly looked old enough to need shaving. His right hand was resting on his gun, his left on his hip. He looked pretty pleased with himself.

He jerked his rotund face toward the back of my Hummer. "And what d'yall think you're doing?"

His voice was pleasant enough; his smile was anything but.

I'm gonna be upfront here. I'm not a big guy. Not physically anyway. Although I used to be. In fact, there was a time when some people used to call me "Big Daddy."

I might not be that big anymore, but I'm not scared of anyone or anything. And, I don't intimidate easy either, not even when the person trying to do the intimidating is a 6' 3" cop who weighs in at around 280 pounds and has his hand resting on a gun.

I squinted up at the guy. "Where the fuck've you been?"

That took him by surprise. It wasn't what he'd been expecting. He thought he'd caught a jewel thief red-handed, in the act, *in flagrante delicto*. What he got instead was a jewelry store owner whose place had just been robbed, and who was madder than a colony of hornets whose nest has just been destroyed.

"My son called the cops about a robbery at my store hours ago," I jabbed at his chest with my index finger. "How come it took you so long to get here? What fucking donut shop were you in? My store was robbed. Don't you care?"

The cop took a step backwards. I wasn't sure if he was taken aback by what I'd said or just trying to avoid being jabbed by my finger again.

He held up his hands. "OK, sir. I understand you're angry. What's your name?"

"Sergio," I scowled. "Sergio Pages. I own Sergio's Jewelry." I pointed to my store. "You know? The place that got robbed last night?"

The officer ignored my sarcasm. "OK, Mr. Pages, let's go take a look at your store, shall we?"

"About fucking time, too." I slammed the tailgate of my truck shut, locked it and led the cop into the store.

I had to hand it to the cop—Officer Donut Shop as I called him—he acted pretty quick once he saw the inside of the store. He called in on his radio and told the dispatcher there had been a burglary at Sergio's Jewelry at Gunn and Casey, and that he needed someone from the Major Crimes Unit there fast. He spoke quickly, his voice terse. When he was done, he looked up at me. Or rather down at me.

"I need to secure this crime scene." He was all business now. "Did anyone touch anything?"

I shrugged. "My son, Sergio Junior, opened up this morning. I came straight in when he called me and told me about the burglary. I checked out the back room and the safes. But, I didn't touch much else. I don't know about Serge and Little Annie."

Officer Donut Shop inclined his chin at the double swing doors. "That the back room?"

I nodded.

"Either of you touch anything?" He was talking to Sergio Junior and Little Annie now.

Serge Junior cleared his throat. "I unlocked the door and realized right away that we'd been robbed. I called 911."

"From the store phone?"

Serge shook his head. Some of his thick black hair fell into his eyes. He pushed it away with his fingers. "I used my cell. Then I called dad. Little Annie arrived while I was making the call. We waited in here for you all to arrive. We didn't touch anything."

"OK." Donut Shop stood, hands on hips, and looked around the store. "I need you three to wait outside until the officers from Major Crimes get here."

He shepherded us out into the bright January sunshine and we stood awkwardly on the sidewalk, trying to ignore the openly curious stares of the passersby as the officer put yellow 'Police Do Not Cross' tape over the doorway.

I sank to the sidewalk and buried my head in my hands as the adrenaline ran out and reality started to sink in. I thought about the $200,000 worth of jewelry that customers, some of whom I'd known for years, had brought in for repair and which had now been stolen.

I knew I was massively underinsured and felt sick to the pit of my stomach. "Oh my God, I am fucked. I am so fucking fucked."

Little Annie came and sat beside me. She hugged me. She'd been the first person I'd worked for in the jewelry industry and, even though she now worked for me, she still thought it was the other way around. She was like a mother to me and the kids, and she worried about us the same way a mother worries about her children.

"Can they go home?" I nodded at Little Annie and Sergio Junior as I asked Officer Donut Shop the question. "It doesn't make any sense for them to hang around here."

The cop nodded. He made sure he took their names and addresses before letting them leave.

"Are you sure you don't need me for anything, Sergio?" Little Annie gave me another hug. "I can stay, if you want me to."

Sergio Junior nodded. "Me too, Dad."

I shook my head. "Go home. There's nothing you can do. There's nothing anyone can do."

I closed my eyes and leaned back against the wall. In the space of four short months, I'd lost pretty much everything I'd ever cared about. First, Theresa and, along with her, my daughter and my own parents, who'd sided with her. And now, my store and my livelihood. I buried my face in my hands and did the only thing I could think of doing. I prayed.

CHAPTER TWO

"Mr. Pages?"

It was a man's voice. Deep and rasping. A man who'd smoked a few too many cigarettes.

"Mr. Pages? Sir? I'm Detective Sergeant Gibson and this is Detective Rebecca T. Ward."

There was a pause. Then, "Mr. Pages, can you hear me?"

I looked up, squinting against the sun that was shining straight into my eyes. Detective Sergeant Gibson stood towering over me. He was built like a linebacker—at least six-two tall and around 250 pounds—but he looked and dressed like a used-car salesman. His short, curly hair was a little too black and perfectly groomed. His face was tanned and smooth, and he was wearing a lot of gold jewelry, although it looked like good-quality stuff. He was also wearing way too much cologne.

I'm good with faces and realized I knew him. He'd been in the store a couple of times. I tried to remember whether he'd bought anything or had just been looking.

The woman standing beside him was short and slight, but perfectly proportioned. Her honey-blonde hair glistened in the sun, giving her a halo that made her look positively angelic. Her bright blue eyes, which were set in a sharp, fair-colored face that was untouched by makeup, were anything but angelic. Despite the situation, I found myself thinking that she was like a piece of candy. You can put me in handcuffs anytime, baby. I nearly said it out loud.

I sighed and rubbed my face with my fingers, before straightening my legs and pushing myself upright.

"Yeah," I was still seething and didn't bother to hide it. "I'm Sergio Pages. Are you the major-crimes detectives? Took you long enough to get here, didn't it?"

"We got here as soon as we could," it was Gibson who answered, no trace of emotion in his voice. "Hey, did that diamond star I was going to buy get stolen, too?"

"What?" That hadn't been what I'd been expecting him to say. "Uh, yes. Almost everything's gone. They cleaned me out."

"Shit, I should have bought it when I had the chance." He pinched the bridge of his nose. "OK, can you tell us what happened?"

"Isn't it obvious? My fucking store got robbed. That's what happened."

Gibson took a deep breath. I could almost hear him mentally counting to ten. "We realize that, Mr. Pages, that's why we're here. Listen, I'm the head of the major-crimes department and I really don't usually respond to cases. But, when I realized this was your store, I decided to take the case. I know what you do for the community. And I wanna help you out here, but I need some details if we're gonna find out who did this. So, when did you first discover you'd been robbed?"

I shook my head to clear it. "I didn't. My son Sergio Junior did. He works for me and opens the store a couple of days a week. Today was one of his days. He called me at home to tell me about the robbery. I came straight here."

"And where is he? Your son, that is?"

I shrugged and jerked my thumb at Officer Donut Shop. "Uh, I asked that cop over there if he and my assistant, Little Annie, could go home. Didn't seem much point in them hanging around. Listen, I already told the other cop all this stuff."

Gibson frowned. "Do you know where your son was last night?"

22

"Shouldn't you be trying to catch the assholes who robbed my store rather than asking me where my son was?"

"We've called the CSI team," Gibson gazed away across the parking lot for a moment before returning his gaze to my face. His sunglasses were totally dark and it was impossible to see where his eyes were actually looking. "Not much we can do until they're finished, so we might as well go through all the background information."

"What about you? Where were you last night?" It was the first time Ward had spoken and I liked the sound of her voice. It was husky with the slightest trace of a Texas accent. I glanced at her. She was writing in a black notebook.

"I was out last night."

"Where?"

"At a poker game."

"Who was with you?"

"Some of my buddies. We're all Rough Riders."

"Rough Riders?" Gibson frowned. "What're Rough Riders? A football team or something?"

I opened my mouth to answer, but Ward beat me to it.

"You know, they're the guys who dress up in army uniforms from a hundred years ago or something. They go round hospitals handing out teddy bears to sick kids. You remember Captain Mangione?"

Gibson nodded.

"He was a Rough Rider. They're like the Elks or the Masons or something."

"Not exactly like the Elks or the Masons," I challenged. "We don't only give teddy bears to sick kids, we also do a lot of other community and charity stuff. Not so long ago a bunch of us built this house for this grandma who was taking care of her grandkids. And, we have floats in parades and hand out beads and things to children and old folks."

"Yeah," Gibson agreed drily. "And you also have poker games. So, tell me about the game last night. Did you win? What time did you get there?"

I shrugged. "We weren't playing for money and I got there about ten-thirty."

"What time did you leave?"

"I don't know."

"You don't know?" Ward sounded skeptical. "What time was it when you got home?"

I shook my head. "I really don't know. Some of the guys and me went to Elmer's after the game. It's right by the club house. We were doing shots. I don't remember much."

"Too many shots to be able to see the clock?" she smiled at Gibson. "So, how did you get home? I hope you didn't drive?"

"Of course not," the words came out more sharply than I'd intended. I was starting to feel pretty stupid. "Someone drove me."

"Who? Would they be able to confirm what time you left?"

I shook my head. Now I felt more than stupid. "I don't know."

"What was the person's name?"

I gazed at the toes of my shoes. "I don't know."

I could almost hear her rolling her eyes. "Do you at least know if it was a man or a woman?"

"It was a woman."

Ward and Gibson shared a look. "So, let me see if I have this right. Some woman drove you home, but you don't know who she was or what her name was?"

Gibson removed his sunglasses. His eyes were brown, the left one a slightly darker shade than the right. It gave him a lopsided appearance. A frown crumpled his face for a nanosecond and vanished. He seemed unaware of it.

"Tell me, Mr. Pages, are you in the habit of going home with women who are complete strangers to you and whose names you don't even know?"

"It wasn't like that."

"Really?" I could tell Ward didn't believe me. "Why don't you tell us what it was like, then?"

I stuck my hands in my pockets. "I need a coffee. If you're quite finished cross-examining me?"

Ward smiled and closed her notebook. "Sure, Mr. Pages. We can talk again later."

I really did need a coffee but, more than that, I needed to get away from Ward. I didn't like the slightly mocking undertone in her voice or the way she looked at me. Shit. I could feel her eyes on the back of my neck as I quickly crossed the plaza to the bar on the other side. They burned.

I liked the bar across the plaza, and drank and ate there often, but I don't think I'd ever been happier to walk into the place. It was dark inside. Comforting and smelling of old cigarettes and stale booze.

26

I slumped down on a stool by the bar as Mick, the owner, appeared. His shirtsleeves were rolled up to his elbows and he had a bar cloth tucked into the belt of his jeans.

"Hey, Sergio! What the hell's going on at your place?"

Mick and I have known each other since high school. He's tall and balding, and wears what remains of his hair pulled back into a long ponytail. He leaned his large, tattooed forearms on the bar top. "What's up with all the cops?"

"My place got robbed last night."

"Fuck." Mick grabbed a couple of shot glasses and filled them with Wild Turkey 101. He slid one across the bar to me. "You all right?"

I picked up the glass and emptied it in a single gulp. "They pretty much cleaned me out, Mick. They cut open all three vaults. There's just about nothing left. It's like a bomb site in there. There's broken glass all over the place and the office is flooded." I placed the glass carefully back onto the bar top. "And all the fucking cops seem to want to do is ask questions about where I was last night. It's like they're not even interested in looking for whoever did this."

"You're kidding me."

I stared into the bottom of my glass and shook my head. "I wish I was."

Mick thumped my back and refilled the glass. "C'mon Serge. You're a fighter. If you can deal with losing all that weight and with losing Theresa, too, you can definitely deal with this. This is a picnic compared to that."

I downed the amber liquid. I wasn't sure he was right about it being a picnic, but he was right about the weight.

Not that long ago, I'd weighed more than 400 pounds. I'd tried dieting so many times, but nothing worked. Sometimes, I went on a diet and put on weight. Then, I had gastric-bypass surgery and lost more than 275 pounds. Saying it like that makes it sound an awful lot easier than it actually was. Like I had an operation and, all of a sudden, I was thin. It was far from that simple. Apart from constantly watching what I ate, I ran four-and-a-half miles, six days a week for more than a year and a half. It was hard work. And I still have to exercise regularly and watch what I eat. It's become a necessary part of my life. That doesn't mean I enjoy it though.

"Sergio?" Mick's voice brought me back to the here and now.

"Fuck it," I put the glass down and got up. "If the cops aren't going to do anything, I will."

"What?"

"I'm going to do what those cops should be doing. I'm going to talk to some of the other store owners and see if anyone saw anything. And, I'm going to take a look around the parking lot, too."

I pulled a twenty from my wallet to pay for the drinks. Mick motioned me to put it away.

He picked up the two shot glasses and started to wash them. "Joe will be in soon. He was working last night. I'll ask him if he saw anything. And, then I'll come and help you."

"Thanks Mick." I was touched by his offer of help. He was a good guy and I knew I was lucky to have him as a friend.

Back out in the parking lot, I looked around the strip mall, trying to decide where to begin. Next door to my shop was a store that sold cell phones. I figured it was as good a place to start as any, but, when I got there, it was all closed up. I rattled the door and knocked loudly. Nothing. I waited a little while, then knocked again, harder this time. I cupped my hands round my eyes and peered through the large glass window. The inside of the store was dark and motionless. If someone was in there, he or she was doing a damn fine job of hiding. It was weird that the store was still closed this late in the day, though. It wasn't like it was a holiday or anything.

A tap on my shoulder made me jump. I spun around. It was Mick.

"Joe just came in. You should come hear what he has to say."

I frowned, but could see Mick wasn't about to elaborate. Whatever it was that Joe had told him, he wanted me to hear it from Joe.

Joe's a small guy like me. At five-foot-eight, I'm not exactly short, but Joe was one of the few guys I knew that I didn't have to literally look up to. Like me, he has a shaved head and diamond stud in one ear. In fact, I'd sold it to him. He was also divorced and the kind of guy that nobody wants to disrespect. Neither of us is a tough ass, but we also don't take shit from anybody. Unlike me, though, he was pale while I only had to glance at the Tampa sun to tan. It was my Cuban and Puerto Rican genes. I'm proud of those genes.

I shook his hand across the bar. His was a firm handshake. "Mick said you had something to tell me?"

Joe tapped a cigarette from his pack and lit it. "Yep. Last night, me and some of the guys noticed a car parked at the back of the parking lot, y'know? It was there for a long time and was still there when I shut up for the night. We figured it was kids..."

He took a long pull on the cigarette making the lit end glow bright red. "Making out, y'know? I saw the tops of two heads. They had the seats reclined all the way back? I thought some lucky bastard was getting a blow job or something?

When Mick told me about your place being ripped off last night, it got me to thinking that maybe the people in that car had something to do with it?"

I pulled my sunglasses from my face and rubbed my eyes. The headache had gone, but my eyes felt suddenly very tired and dry. "How do you mean?"

"Well, I'm figuring that whoever was parked in that car would have had a perfect view of all of the stores? And would certainly have been able to warn anyone in your place if someone arrived or if the cops or security guys turned up to do a patrol. I'm thinking that it might have been a look-out car or something?"

Joe has a way of talking that makes it sound like every other sentence is a question.

I spun around on my bar stool and stared out the large window. If the cops were intending to search the parking lot, they hadn't shown any sign of starting yet. I could see people driving by and slowing down to stare at the store and the yellow 'Police Do Not Cross' tape across the door and around the sidewalk.

"Can you show me where the car was parked?"

Joe nodded.

We walked across the parking lot.

"There," Joe pointed to a place at the back of the lot. "That's where it was?"

I could see Joe was right. Whoever had parked there certainly would have been able to easily see all the entrances and exits to the mall, as well as having an excellent view of my shop. If the thieves had a look-out, this is definitely where he or she would have parked.

Joe lit another cigarette from the butt of his existing one. He crushed the finished cigarette beneath his heel. He jerked his head toward something on the pavement. "What's that?"

I went to check out what Joe had seen and found a small pile of cigarette butts and an empty milk carton. Skimmed. Whoever drank it must have been worried about their weight. I crouched down to get a better look, being careful not to touch anything.

"Do you think these could have been left by the people in that car last night?

Joe sucked on his cigarette. "This is exactly where the car was parked, so anything dropped out of the driver's side window or door would have been left right about there."

I clapped him on the back. "Thanks, Joe. I'll go tell the cops. You mind waiting here and making sure that no one parks or disturbs that stuff until someone comes to collect it?"

"Yup?"

I crossed the parking lot back toward my store, feeling more hopeful than when I'd walked into Mick's place. The cop at the door didn't want to let me in, but relented when I explained who I was. Gibson and Ward were in the back office, ankle deep in water. I realized that my shoes, socks and feet were still soaking from when I'd been in there earlier. I hadn't even noticed until now.

Ward must have heard me sloshing across the store because she glanced up and nudged Gibson who turned to look in my direction. He smoothed a perfectly manicured hand across his hair before intercepting me at the door to the office.

"Mr. Pages, what can we do for you?"

"Did you find anything?"

Gibson held up his hands. "This is an ongoing police investigation, Mr. Pages, and I'm afraid that I really can't tell you anything at the moment."

I felt the heat rise in my face. "This is my—"

"I know," Gibson didn't let me finish. "And the best thing you can do is let us do our jobs. Now, was there something you wanted?"

I told him about the car that had been parked in the parking lot the night before, the pile of cigarette ends and the empty milk carton.

Gibson pursed his lips, then shrugged. "Maybe something, maybe nothing. We'll check it out."

I don't know what reaction I was expecting, but this definitely wasn't it.

"Fuck it." I could hear my voice rising in pitch and volume. "You cops haven't even looked in the parking lot yet. And, with all the cars coming and going any evidence is being destroyed. The least you can do is fucking check this stuff out. Maybe there was a look-out in that car, and maybe that person left that stuff behind."

"OK, OK." Ward spoke soothingly, but more than a little patronizingly. "We'll get a CSI to check out the place where your friend says he saw the car parked. OK?"

She turned to one of the white-suited CSIs and muttered a few words. The CSI nodded and headed in the direction of the parking lot.

"Happy now?" Ward's face was inscrutable. "You have to understand that the water in here is damaging and destroying a lot of evidence. We're not ignoring the parking lot or what's outside, we're merely prioritizing. And, right now, collecting whatever evidence is left in here is more important."

She was lecturing me and we both knew it. Strangely enough, I quite liked it. I found myself thinking about those handcuffs again.

"Was there anything else, Mr. Pages?"

I shoved my hands deep into my pockets, biting back the answer I felt like giving her. They were condescending bastards, but it wouldn't serve any purpose to further antagonize her or Gibson. "I did try to talk to the owner of the cell phone store next door, but he's not there and the store is all closed up."

Ward shrugged. "Maybe he just slept in?"

I shook my head and felt the headache start to pound again. I needed more Tylenol. "He's always open on time. You can set your watch by him. I was just thinking that maybe he had something to do with the robbery. I happen to know he has a good buddy who's a coke dealer."

Gibson snorted derisively. Ward buried her face in her hands. "Look Mr. Pages—"

"Sergio." I interrupted.

She sighed. "Look Sergio, you can't go around accusing people of being involved in the robbery just because they turn up late for work and happen to have a friend who might or might not be a drug dealer."

I could feel my face burning. "It's really unusual for him not to open up his store. I've never known it to happen before."

"Sergio, calm down," Ward was using a voice I figured she usually saved for recalcitrant children and old people. "We'll check out the owner of the store next door, OK? It's standard practice anyway. Now, please go away and leave us to do our job."

I forced myself to take a couple of steadying breaths and unclench my fists as I turned to leave. As I did so, I caught sight of the peg board in my office.

"My tickets are gone."

Ward followed my gaze to the board. "What?"

"I had four tickets to the hockey game this weekend pinned to the board. Right there." I pointed to where the tickets had been.

Ward wrote something in her notebook. "We'll look into it."

"Fuck this shit."

The room went quiet. Everyone turned to stare at me. Ward and Gibson shared a look, and then Ward grabbed my elbow and had manhandled me out into the parking lot before I knew what was happening.

"Listen to me," her voice was low and hard. "And, listen good because I don't have all day and I am not about to repeat myself. I have a job to do and I'm doing it the best way I can. If you don't like it, tough fucking luck. You're in the way and you need to leave. Now. We'll check out the owner of the cell phone store, and we will check out your missing hockey tickets. Do you remember the seat numbers?"

I folded my arms across my chest as I told her the section, row and seat numbers.

Ward wrote the information down in her notebook. "Thank you. Now, go home and leave this to the experts."

CHAPTER THREE

I was angry. So I did what I did whenever I got angry or sad or lonely these days: I went to my favorite bar and got drunk. Very drunk. It wasn't hard. People had heard about the robbery and were buying me drinks and commiserating. I closed the place, like I had so many times before in the months since Theresa had left, and staggered out into the moonlight.

I weaved unsteadily down the street, stumbled and grabbed onto a streetlight to stop myself from falling. I spun around, coming to rest less than gracefully on the sidewalk, my back against the lamppost. I leaned my head back, trying to stop the sensation that the world around me was spinning out of control. The whirling pit. I hated that about being drunk. I knew if I stayed put until everything stopped moving, I'd be OK. But, I had no idea how long that might take.

I watched the cars and trucks drive along the street. It struck me that it would be quite easy to get up and fall in front of one, preferably one of the bigger trucks. The traffic was moving quite fast and I was sure that death would be pretty instantaneous. My blood-alcohol level was such that they'd almost certainly say it was an accident rather than suicide, too, which would mean that my kids would still get my insurance payout. Right then, right there, it was a surprisingly attractive thought.

Quick, easy, dead.

Nothing more to worry about. No more agonizing about the $500,000 I still owed Theresa or the $200,000-worth of customers' jewelry that had been in the store for repair, not to mention the $150,000 I owed wholesalers for the other jewelry that had been stolen. No more fretting about the broken air conditioner at home or the leak in my roof or the problems with my Hummer. No more worrying about how the hell I was going to pay for any of that now that my business was gone. Life really couldn't get much worse.

A truck rumbled past and I felt the hot blast of its wake on my face. I pushed myself away from the lamppost toward the traffic.

"Hey Sergio. That you?"

I twisted my head to see where the voice was coming from and was transfixed by an angel. I tried to speak, but no words came out. No intelligible words anyway.

The angel finally came into focus and I saw it was Mo, who worked at the bar. Mo was a riot. She was in her fifties and had tightly curled redder-than-red hair and the biggest chest I'd ever seen. She always wore low-cut shirts that showed off her magnificent breasts and skirts that were short and tight. She had a big heart, too.

"Sergio?" She placed a hand gently on my shoulder. I noticed all of the rings, several on each finger and thumb, as well as her bony knuckles and bent fingers. It was funny, I'd never noticed her fingers before. I wondered if someone had broken them for her. "You look like you could use a ride home, hon."

Words came out of my mouth, but I didn't understand them and I don't think that she did either.

She laughed and grabbed my arms, pulling me upright and supporting me toward her car, which was parked a little way along the curb. "C'mon, hon. Let's get you home."

She got me into the car and put the seat belt on me, and then chain smoked as she drove me home. She rolled the passenger-side window right down even though it wasn't that warm.

"Don't want you throwing up in my car," she explained with a grin.

She chattered and smoked as she drove. It was quite a feat of multi-tasking. Both hands on the steering wheel, cigarette dangling from one corner of her mouth as she spoke. Every so often, she'd take the cigarette from her mouth and knock the ash from it before replacing it between her lips.

I didn't really listen to what she was saying, until she pulled up in front of my house. "The interesting thing, though, is that when you're down and out, there's really only one way to go. And that's up."

She glanced at me as if I'd heard the entire story and not just the last two sentences. I nodded and climbed unsteadily out of her car. It didn't matter what the rest of her story was. She was right. From here, there was only one way. And that was up.

I was going to get over my bitch of an ex-fucking-wife, save my store and put my life back together. Then, I was going to go hunting, but not for white-tailed deer at my place in Alabama. I was going hunting for the bastards who'd robbed my place. And, when I found them, and I would find them, we were going to have a nice private party at my cabin in the woods. Payback is a motherfucker and I was going to pay those bastards back if it was the last thing I ever did. It would definitely be the last thing they ever did. What goes around, comes around. And, sooner or later all the people who had screwed me over were going to get theirs.

I love karma; she's a fucking bitch.

The hammering on the front door that woke me the following morning was replaced by a softer, but more insistent, tapping on my bedroom door a few minutes later.

"Mmmmmh?" I looked at the clock. It was past ten. I'd overslept again.

Sergio Junior's face peered around the door. "Uh, Dad? The cops are here. The ones from yesterday morning. They want to talk to you."

I pushed myself up on one elbow and nodded, my mouth too dry to make any words. Recognizable ones, anyway. I waved at him to go away and crawled out of bed, pulled on the jeans that were lying on the floor and went into the bathroom to douse my face with cold water. I got to the kitchen to find that my son had already put on a pot of coffee. I poured a cup and joined Gibson and Ward who were sitting at the kitchen table.

"So?" I muttered.

Gibson placed his coffee mug carefully on the table. "We wanted to talk to you a little more about the robbery at your store."

"Uh huh?"

"Did you have any luck remembering who the woman was who brought you home?"

I gulped the coffee and scalded my mouth. "You know, I think she left her panties here. Would you like me to go get them for you so you can check them for DNA? I know, here's an idea, you could do that at the same time you're checking those cigarette butts and milk carton for DNA. Then, maybe you won't even need to see if anyone uses those hockey tickets."

"Don't be like that, Sergio," Ward snapped. "You're not helping anyone and certainly not yourself."

I met her steady blue gaze. "I wasn't aware I had to help myself. I'm the victim here, aren't I?"

Ward looked away first, glancing down at her hands, which were wrapped around her coffee mug. No ring I noticed. "We have to check out everything. And everyone."

"What the fuck?" I scowled at Gibson. "You know me, man, you shopped at my store. You know the stuff I do for the community. I can't believe you are seriously suspecting me."

Gibson cleared his throat. "Yeah, but it's not like we've ever broken bread together or anything. And, like Ward said, we have to check out everyone."

"Yeah, sure, it just looks like you're concentrating on me. And, while you're doing that, the trail to the real thieves is getting cold."

Gibson checked his notebook. "We understand you were recently divorced, Mr. Pages."

I was still 'Mr. Pages' to him. "Yeah, she left me and the boys back in September. My daughter had already left home."

"Was it amicable?"

"Or expected?" Ward chimed in.

I stared away through the kitchen window. It was cloudy today and looked like it might even rain later. A big change from the weather of the day before.

"Mr. Pages?" Gibson's voice brought me back into the kitchen.

I shrugged. "It wasn't expected. I had no idea there was anything wrong until the day she left. I guess it was amicable though. If by amicable you mean that I gave her half of everything without a lawyer."

In the silence that followed, I could hear birds singing down by the water at the end of the yard. Their melodic cries mingled with the noise of Gibson fiddling with his loose change.

The detective pulled his hand from his pocket and the chinking noise stopped. "Do you think there's any chance your ex-wife might have had something to do with the robbery? Maybe she needed money or wanted to hurt you or something by destroying your business?"

I stared at him.

"What about the divorce settlement?" Gibson continued evenly. "It must have cost you a lot to pay your ex-wife half of everything. And, we also understand that you recently needed to make repairs to your Hummer's transmission and the roof of your house. How did you find that kind of money? Tell me, Mr. Pages, do you have an insurance policy on the store? What's it worth?"

I had to hand it to him, he and Ward had done their homework. It was scary how they'd managed to find out so much about me in such a short space of time.

Ward must have seen the storm clouds gathering on my face because she jumped in before I could say a word. "We have to explore all the options, Sergio."

"Yeah," I snarled, getting to my feet. "All the options that involve me or a member of my family being responsible for the robbery. I don't see you exploring any other options. For your fucking information, I was under-insured by about a million dollars. I just lost 20 years of profit in one fucking night. Do you seriously think I pulled this thing off for the insurance money? Fucking assholes." I muttered the last two words under my breath.

I crossed the kitchen and poured more coffee into my mug. My hands were shaking.

"I can assure you, Mr. Pages, that we are exploring all of the possibilities in this case." Gibson's voice was calm, almost monotone.

"You damn well don't seem to be exploring any possibilities with as much energy as you're putting into me and my family." My face was as hot as my coffee. "I'm sorry I don't know who I was with the night my store was robbed, but you can be one-hundred-percent certain that I had nothing to do with it. And neither did my son or my ex-wife. I'll even take a lie detector test to prove it, if you want."

Again, that look flashed between Ward and Gibson before they both got to their feet. I wondered for a fleeting moment if they were telepathic.

"Thank you for your time, Mr. Pages." It was Gibson who concluded the interview. "We'll be in touch."

I didn't see them to the door.

After they left, I sat and took one deep breath after another, trying to rid myself of the feelings of anger and helplessness. I hated that I had absolutely no control over the situation I was in.

"Are we gonna be OK, Dad?" Sergio Junior joined me at the table. "Maybe I ought to go look for a job or something? To help out until you get back on your feet?"

I put my hand over his and squeezed.

"We're gonna be OK, Serge," I growled with a lot more conviction than I felt. "Your dad's like a phoenix. You wait and see. We're going to find the bastards who robbed the store and we're gonna prove to those damn cops that we had nothing to do with it."

I was as low as I'd ever been. I'd lost everything I cared about and my life sucked, but at least I had a purpose. I realized I hadn't felt this energized since before Theresa had left me. It was a good feeling.

I'm the first to admit that I'm not the smartest guy when it comes to reading and writing. Hell, I don't even know my addition or multiplication tables. But, I know people. And, I know about the world. I know about life, too. Everything I have, I earned. And I earned it the hard way.

I figured there were two things I could do to prove my innocence and get a lead on the assholes who burglarized my store. First, I could try and find the woman I'd been with that night and get her to give me an alibi. Hell, it was even possible she was an accomplice to the robbers, sent to keep me occupied while they ripped off my place.

Second, I could get into that hockey game on Saturday night and see who turned up and sat in my seats.

I showered and dressed, and drove into town. Rain had started to fall out of a sky that was sullen and bruised like a street fighter who's had the crap kicked out of him. I turned on the wipers and the air conditioning as I tried to remember which of Rough Riders had been at the poker game that night. I knew Derrick, George, Mike and Richey had been there for sure because they were playing at the same table as me. I decided to start with Derrick Delarosa who ran his own real-estate business.

It took me a while to find a place to park. The Hummer's big and there wasn't a space large enough on Main Street. I circled around and eventually found a place on one of the tree-lined side streets about a block from Derrick's office. The rain was easing off, but I still got pretty damp as I jogged quickly across the street and around the corner, trying to avoid the puddles. I shook the rain from my jacket as I pushed through the door and grinned at Derrick's receptionist. Monica's a baby doll. Tall with curves in all the right places. If I was ten years younger and she wasn't married, I'd have made a play for her.

"Serge!"

The only downside to Monica was her voice, which, unlike her, had never grown up. It was high pitched and made her sound far too much like a ten-year-old kid. One of those voices that made people ask if mom or dad were home when they called up on the phone.

"I was real sorry to hear about your store, Serge. That's a bummer." She came round the desk and gave me a hug. It felt damn good.

"Thanks, sweetheart. Derrick in?"

"Yep." She jerked her thumb in the direction of a door marked 'Derrick Delarosa – Owner'.

"Thanks."

She flashed a mouthful of perfectly straight, gleaming white teeth at me and giggled. "You're welcome."

I knocked on the door and pushed it open without waiting for a reply.

I liked Derrick Delarosa. He was about twenty years older than me and suffered from angina, and life had been tough on him in the past couple of years, but he was a good man all the same.

"Sergio." As always Derrick seemed genuinely happy to see me. But then, Derrick usually seemed genuinely happy to see everyone. "I heard about what happened at your store. What can I do to help? You need money?"

That was typical of Derrick. He'd give you his last dime or the shirt off his back if you needed it.

I shook my head and dropped into the chair on the opposite side of his desk. "How're you doing, Derrick?"

He didn't look well. His face and big dome of a head were grey and covered with a light sheen of sweat. He was wheezing heavily, like he'd just run up a couple of flights of stairs. That's pretty normal for Derrick, though.

He shrugged and held up his hands. "I think I should be asking you that."

I leaned forward, resting my forearms on the desk. "You remember the poker game the other night?"

Derrick's snort of laughter quickly turned into a cough that didn't stop. He pulled a handkerchief from his pocket, waving away my attempts to help him. The door to the office opened and Monica came in carrying a glass of water, which she placed on the desk in front of him before disappearing back into the reception area. Eventually the paroxysm of coughing stopped. Derrick took some sips of water and dabbed at his watering eyes.

"Damn heart," he muttered.

He took a couple of breaths. "Yep, I remember that poker game. I lost and so did you."

He chuckled again and quickly sipped some water to preempt the coughing fit that might follow.

"Did you see who took me home?"

Derrick frowned at the ceiling and then slowly shook his balding head. "I left when you and the guys headed over to Elmer's. My damn doc don't like me drinking. You were pretty drunk by the end of the game though. I hope you didn't drive?"

"Nah. A woman took me home. A blonde-haired beauty. She was all legs. Did you happen to see her?"

Derrick picked up his spectacles from the desk and put them on his face. "You always did have a way with the ladies. There wercn't any women at the poker game though, blonde or otherwise. You know me, I would've noticed if there had been women there. It was just the regular guys. George, Mike and Richey at our table, and then I think that Allan, Pete, Zach and Hugo were there, too. Maybe a couple of the other guys. You must have met your beautiful blonde when you and the guys went to Elmer's."

I had to smile. Derrick was right, he would have noticed if there had been any women at the poker game. He was lonely and looking for someone to share his life, and he tended to notice any and all women wherever he was.

"Why do you ask?"

I shrugged. "The police seem to think I had something to do with the robbery and I need to find that woman who took me home. She's the only alibi I've got. I also figured that it's possible she was working with the robbers. And that maybe she took me home to make sure I stayed out of the way all night."

"The police think you had something to do with the robbery at your store? Are they crazy?" Rick pulled open a desk drawer and rummaged in it. Eventually he came up with a business card. He pushed it across the desk in my direction. "That's my lawyer. Damn fine one too. Call her if you need any legal advice, OK?"

I picked up the card and pushed it into my wallet without looking at it. "Thanks Derrick. I appreciate it."

It had stopped raining, but a chill wind had picked up. I turned up the collar of my coat. I was suddenly very cold and very tired. The fact that Derrick couldn't even remember seeing the blonde babe left me inexplicably disappointed. Shit. I wasn't a cop or a private detective, and if I couldn't even find anyone who'd seen the woman who took me home, how the hell was I ever going to find the people who'd hit my store? I was stupid to think I could. A private detective though, now there was an idea. I dismissed it quickly. I had no money for anything, and definitely not for a private detective.

The lights in the diner half-way down the street shone through the gloom of the miserable day. I jogged quickly toward it. I could at least afford a cup of coffee.

A bell jingled as I pushed through the door. The place was half empty. The people who were there were mostly seniors or mothers with babies in strollers. I chose a table by the window, as far away from other customers as possible, and sat down.

"What can I get you, hon?" The waitress filled the cup on the table with coffee from a jug without being asked. She pulled her notepad from a pocket in her off-white apron and licked the end of her pencil, and then looked at me expectantly. As her hazel eyes met mine, her face broke into a smile of recognition. "Aren't you Sergio from Sergio's Jewelry?"

I nodded and smiled. I pay a lot for the TV commercials I make and I love it when someone remembers me from one of them.

"I'm Carly," she offered. "Carly McMillan. Remember? We danced together at the L.A. Hangout?" She elbowed me good naturedly as she tucked some strands of graying hair back into place behind her ear. "It's nice to be around guys who aren't afraid to get up and dance."

She tilted her head to one side. "I heard about the robbery at your store. I'm sorry."

So, she didn't know me from my commercials after all. I shrugged. "Shit happens."

She chuckled. "Tell me about it."

She had a good-natured laugh.

"Anyhow, anytime you want a good time, you come see me." She winked. "You know what I mean?"

I grinned despite myself. "Yeah, I know what you mean."

"So. What'll it be?"

I smiled at her as I thought for a minute. Keeping my weight down wasn't easy despite the surgery, and I like food. And sex. "How's about bacon and eggs sunny side up with rye toast on the side. And no butter. And then, I was thinking about maybe having you for dessert. What d'ya think of that order?"

She threw back her head and laughed. "Good choice. I like to think we have the best damn dessert in town." She blew me an air kiss and walked away with an exaggerated wiggle that widened my smile.

I stirred my spoon idly through my coffee as I stared through the rain-smeared window at the miserable January day. I watched a large man and his equally large wife waddle down the sidewalk together. I momentarily wondered if they were happy and if they made wild love every day like me and Theresa used to do when I still had a 64-inch waist.

Before I'd had the surgery and gotten thin, I'd been as large as the guy walking down the street, maybe even larger. I remembered taking off my belt one day and realizing it was taller than I was. I was wider around the waist than I was tall. But, Theresa and I had never had any problems making love despite my weight. We had a good sex life. A very good sex life. Shit, I'd thought we had a good life, period. She'd obviously thought differently though.

I still missed her like crazy. She was my soul mate, knew me better than anyone ever could. And she was so damn hot. Fuck. Why did she have to leave? What was it she'd said? She still loved me, but she didn't like me anymore? What kind of a reason was that?

I'd gone through gastric-bypass surgery and then worked really hard to lose more than 200 pounds in little more than a year. I thought things would be perfect. It turned out the weight wasn't all I ended up losing.

I still remember what it was like to be morbidly obese. I recall it like it was yesterday. I was always big: Sergio Pages, the larger-than-life guy with the larger-than-life personality. I ate like it was Thanksgiving every day and I'd eaten that way since I was a little kid. By the time I was 42, I couldn't fit into a seat at Raymond James Stadium. My knees were shot because of all the weight I was carrying and I couldn't walk without a cane. I had tendinitis in my wrist from leaning on the cane. I even got chest pains when my tiny wife lay on top of me after we made love.

After the 2003 Super Bowl, when I tried to welcome home the Tampa Bay Buccaneers, a police officer chased me from the bench seat I'd staked out for my family. You know what the cop told me? She said the seats were reserved. Hell, all the seats in the place were free that night, but she gave that bench seat to a skinny little family instead. She said I could sit in the handicapped section, but that my family would have to sit somewhere else. Cold-hearted bitch. I like to think I'm tough so I tried to hide how I felt when the cop made me move, but I cried that night. I stood in front of a seat I was too fat to fit into and I cried. I cried because I was embarrassed for my family. I cried because I was embarrassed for myself. I felt fat and old and miserable, and I hated the way people treated me because of my size.

Everything changed the day my doctor told me I had diabetes, high blood pressure and high cholesterol. He also told me I had a 50-50 chance of dying within five years. Talk about a wake-up call. The very next day, I started my 28th diet, but instead of losing weight, I gained five pounds. That was when I decided on the surgery.

It wasn't an easy decision. I read everything I could about the surgery until I knew the statistics and the risks inside out and upside down. My doctor told me that having the operation could reduce my risk of dying in the next few years by about 40 percent, if I was lucky. But, it's not without risks. Complications after the surgery are common and about two percent of patients die within one month. It also takes a lot of hard work to keep the weight off afterwards. It's not like a magic potion; a miraculous cure for obesity. It's fucking hard work. For me, it was my last chance of living something like a normal life.

Preparing for the surgery was tough, but afterwards was even worse. Imagine being mentally starving. To want to eat, but to be physically unable to do so. That's what it feels like. I had to acclimatize my body to food. I started with the tiniest bits of nourishment, all of it liquid. Even long after the surgery, it was a huge deal to go from eating a tablespoon of tuna to a quarter of a can. And then, there was the exercise, walking further and further every day, never working out less today than I did yesterday, and finally starting to jog short distances until I was running more than four miles every day.

"Here's your bacon and eggs, hon."

I smiled my thanks. The bacon smelled good. There would have been a time after the surgery when I wouldn't have been able to even think about eating something like this, but now I could. It had been a long, hard journey, but here I was 227 pounds lighter and looking, and sometimes even feeling, like a completely different person. I even occasionally refer to myself in the third person.

Women also hit on me nowadays like they'd never done before, when I'd been big, but my beautiful wife, who'd stuck with me through the obesity and the weight-loss surgery, had left me. I still couldn't quite get my head around that; I'd thought life would be perfect once I'd lost weight. Instead, exactly the opposite had happened. Like I always say, though, karma's a bitch and she'd sure had her fun with me, even if I couldn't figure out what I'd done to deserve it.

I was full after eating half of my breakfast. Before the gastric-bypass surgery, I wouldn't have been able to leave unfinished food on my plate. In fact, I probably would have eaten not only that plate of bacon and eggs but one, two or even three more. Today, I pushed the plate away and finished up my coffee.

The rain had stopped and the sun was trying to make an appearance. I paid for my breakfast and handed Carly a generous tip.

"You want a rain check on that dessert?" she grinned.

58

"Absolutely." I meant it, too.

CHAPTER FOUR

I spent the next few days checking in with everyone who'd gone with me to Elmer's after the Rough Riders poker game that night.

Unlike Derrick, they all remembered the woman who'd taken me home, but none of them had ever seen her before or knew who she was. They'd all assumed she was a friend of mine, an assumption given credence by the fact that she'd taken me home. George and Mike had even helped her get me into her car, a beautiful charcoal-grey Corvette C6 convertible. George had fallen in love with the car and was pretty jealous that I'd gotten a ride home in it. Not that I knew anything about it. I'd been out cold. The only one of the guys I wasn't able to talk to was Richey, who was out of town on business until Friday.

In between trying to put a name to the blonde, I met with the insurance adjustor. That was a blast. He told me I was badly underinsured and that there was no way the company would pay out anything as long as I was under suspicion of being involved in the robbery.

The cops didn't seem to be getting anywhere with their investigation either. If anything, it seemed to me like they were focusing more and more on me as their prime suspect and less and less on anyone else. It didn't seem to matter what I said, how often I protested my innocence or how many times I offered to take a lie detector test.

I finally caught up with Richey late on Friday afternoon at O'Brien's, which is the best pub in Tampa, as far as I'm concerned anyway. It's like a second home to me, and Bernie and Teresa, who own the place, had been my customers for more than 18 years. I think Bernie had bought every one of his anniversary presents for his wife at my store.

When I got there, the place was already starting to fill up with the after-work crowd. As I walked in, the small group of guys standing between the door and the bar, nursing drinks and cigarettes, glanced in my direction. They equally quickly resumed their conversation when they saw it was just a guy. They paid a lot more attention to the three women in heels and tight skirts who followed me in.

Only four days had passed since the robbery, but it seemed like a lifetime and then some. I felt like I'd aged a decade for each one of those days.

I craned my head and looked around for Richey as I made my way through the small huddles of people. Finally, I saw him. He was sitting in a booth at the back. I caught the attention of the cute little blond-haired server.

She greeted me with a kiss. "I'm so sorry to hear about what happened to your place, Sergio. That sucks. Can I buy you a drink?"

I nodded my thanks and slid into the seat across from Richey.

"Hey Serge, what was she talking about?" Richey grinned.

I shrugged as the server placed my beer on the table in front of me. "You haven't heard?"

Richey leaned his forearms on the table, carefully avoiding a small pool of spilled alcohol. He shook his head. "Heard what? What's going on? I've been down in the Keys all week fishing and chasing skirt. I've not spoken to anyone."

I picked up my beer and took a gulp. I felt exhausted, worn-out, like someone had pulled my plug and all my energy had swirled noisily down the drain.

"My store got robbed. They pretty much cleaned me out. There's almost nothing left."

I can't remember the last time I cried in front of another person. I was close to it now though.

"What can I do?"

That was typical of Richey. Present him with a problem and he'll ask what he can do to solve it.

I finished my beer. Richey signaled for another round.

"Do you remember the Rough Riders poker night on Monday?"

The expressions chased across Richey's large open face. He could seldom hide what he was thinking and feeling, however hard he tried.

"What does Monday night's poker game have to do with your store being robbed?"

"After the game, we went to Elmer's and did some shots. Remember? There was a woman there. She took me home."

Richcy settled back into the seat. "Uh, I was pretty drunk that night, Serge."

The server brought two more beers. I took mine and downed half of it.

"Yeah, me too." I smiled ruefully. "Anyhow, this chick took me home. Only I can't remember her name or anything else about her."

Richey was shaking his head slowly. "There was a woman. She had long blonde hair and was fucking hot. Why is it all the cute chicks go for you?"

"Because I have a big dick. What do you want me to tell you?"

Richey grinned. "Bastard. But, I have no idea who she was. I never saw her before." He laughed and nudged my arm. "I wouldn't mind seeing her again though, if you know what I mean."

I glanced around the bar. The music had gotten louder. Simon and Garfunkel, Mrs. Robinson. I found my foot tapping in time to the music.

"Yeah," I muttered more to myself than to Richey. "I wouldn't mind seeing her again, too."

"What about the store, Sergio? What can I do to help you? There must be something."

I took a deep breath and shook my head. "There's really nothing anyone can do. However you cut it, I'm royally fucked. I've lost everything and, as if that wasn't enough, the cops think I had something to do with the robbery. I don't think they're even really looking for anyone else."

"That's stupid. How can they even begin to think that you of all people would ever do anything like that?"

"They think it's because of the divorce. That I needed money or something. But even that's a joke because I was underinsured by about a million bucks. And, anyway, the insurance company won't pay out until the police clear me of any involvement. Even if they do pay out, though, I won't get nearly enough to cover all the stolen jewelry."

Richey finished his beer in one swallow. "Shit."

"Yep, Richey. That pretty much sums it up. Fucking shit."

The cops called the next morning to say that they'd finished at the store and I could go back in there and start to clean up. Cleaning up the debris after a robbery was definitely not how I'd been planning to spend my weekend, but then the week had been full of things that wouldn't have been top of my bucket list of things I want to do before I die.

Sergio Junior came with me. We made the drive in silence. When we got to the store, the place looked forlorn and abandoned, the yellow 'Police Do Not Cross' tape fluttering in the slight breeze.

I pulled the tape down and we walked into the store. The chaos was as bad as I remembered it, worse even. There was mess and debris and water everywhere. My heart sank. This was going take weeks to clear up, but I wasn't about to let Sergio Junior see how I felt.

"C'mon kid. Let's get started."

I went into the back to see whether I could salvage any of my records. I'd had a lot of jewelry in the store for repair and the first thing I wanted to do was contact everyone and let them know what had happened. I felt terrible for the people who'd left their jewelry with me to be repaired only to have it stolen. Some of it I remembered and some I did not, but I knew all of it was irreplaceable in terms of memories. I didn't know how I was going to tell people what had happened. To be honest, this was probably what I felt the worst about. I really love my customers. I'd known some of them for years, decades even. They were like family to me. The thought of telling them that their jewelry had been stolen was making me ill. I went into the bathroom and threw up.

It didn't take me long to realize that my laptop had been stolen along with the jewelry. The desktop computer on which I'd stored all of my records had been destroyed and left floating in the scummy water. I guess the thieves didn't want me to have a complete inventory to give to the cops.

"Uh, Dad?" Sergio Junior's voice startled me from my thoughts. "There's some folks here to see you."

I turned around and saw Mr. and Mrs. Galantino. They'd been customers of mine pretty much since I'd started the store more than 20 years before. In fact, after I had the gastric-bypass surgery and became thin, Mrs. Galantino came in and demanded to know where Sergio was and why he'd sold the store without telling anyone. It had been pretty funny explaining to her that she really was still talking to the old Sergio, but it took a while to convince her.

I stepped into what was left of my store and shook hands with each of them. "Mr. and Mrs. Galantino, I'm sorry, but—"

"It's all right, young man." Mrs. Galantino had kept hold of my hand and was patting the back of it as she spoke. "We heard what happened to you. So terrible. Terrible. What is the world coming to? We came to see if there was anything we could do to help."

Mr. Galantino nodded his agreement. "You're like family, Sergio. Tell us what we can do."

I pulled Mrs. Galantino toward me and hugged her. It was either that or start to cry. "Thank you. I can't tell you what it means for you to come all this way to talk to me. But there's really nothing you can do. Except maybe pray?"

The Galantinos smiled at each other and nodded. They knew a lot about praying. "I'll get the rosary out as soon as I get home, Sergio. And we'll ask Father to say a prayer for you at Mass tomorrow. It'll be all right. You'll see. After all, God never puts more on your plate than you can handle, you know."

"I know, but I'm just kind of wondering why he had to pile it so high."

"Because he thinks you still have a big stomach." Mr. Galantino's face was completely straight, then he cracked a smile, and we all laughed.

So it was for the rest of the morning. A constant stream of people coming by the store. Some came to see what was going on, others came and offered their prayers and their help. Buoyed by all of their good wishes, I made up some signs and put them on the door.

"Pray for us," the signs read. "We've been robbed. But we will open again. Nothing and nobody can keep me down."

I meant it too. I believe you only fail if you quit trying And there was no way I was going to quit until I was six feet under.

In between greeting the stream of visitors and waving to the drivers who slowed as they strained to read the signs, I started to make a list of all those people I could remember whose jewelry had been at the store for repair.

At lunchtime, Mick and Joe and some of the regulars from the bar at the other end of the mall came by with sandwiches and beer and more offers of help.

The afternoon brought yet more people and more generosity. One customer, Jimmy Siccarello, who's a local real-estate broker and an old friend from high school, came in with a check for $500.

He said it was to help me out and that I shouldn't worry because this was just a bump in the road. I told him I'd pay him back one day and he said he knew I would.

By the end of the day, despite a lot of hard work by a lot of people, the store was still a complete mess, but I felt like a million bucks.

The evening of the Tampa Bay Lightening game at the St. Pete Times Forum finally rolled around. The one I'd had the great tickets for. The tickets that had been pinned to the peg board at the shop and which had been taken by the thieves. The cops had told me to let them handle things, but I wasn't about to do that. After all, Gibson and Ward hadn't exactly shown that they were on my side in all of this. In fact, I had my doubts as to whether they'd even be there at all to see if anyone came and sat in the seats I'd had tickets for.

I knew that getting into the game myself wasn't going to be easy. My tickets had been stolen and there were none left to buy this close to game time. But, I wasn't going to let a little thing like not having a ticket deter me. I'd figure something out. I always did.

The three decks of the St. Pete Times Forum were crowded with people and buzzing with energy when I got there. I tried the box office first, hoping that they might have some returns, but was out of luck. After that, I wandered around outside for a while to see if anyone was scalping a ticket. It happens sometimes, but not always. There were no scalpers that night though. The place started to empty as people took their seats, and I could hear the music echoing around and the sound of people cheering and shouting and singing and stamping their feet. I felt a rush of adrenaline and wished I was there to just drink beer and watch the game. I love hockey games. There's nothing quite like the excitement of cheering on your team, and definitely nothing like seeing them win. There's also the fact that the best-looking ladies go to hockey games.

Tonight, though, I wasn't here for the game or the ladies. Tonight, I was here to see if anyone was dumb enough to use those tickets of mine. But, I wasn't going to be able to find out if I couldn't get in.

I left the building and started to walk around it, hoping I might find another way in. The sun was sinking fast and there was a chill in the air. I turned up my collar and thrust my hands into my pockets to keep them warm.

On any other evening, I would have enjoyed the beautiful sunset and the fiery red sky, but tonight it barely registered. What was I thinking, driving all the way out here expecting I'd somehow miraculously find a way in. Sometimes I was such a dumb fuck, I surprised even myself at how incredibly stupid I could be. Maybe that was why Theresa had left me.

"Hey Sergio? Sergio Pages?"

I was so deep in thought that it took me a few moments to realize someone was calling my name. I turned. I was around the back of the building now. Standing by some huge dumpsters was a small group of big guys having a smoke.

One of them lifted his cigarette in a greeting. "Sergio!"

He was tall and muscular, his tanned face topped by short dark hair that was buzz cut. I searched for a name to go with the face.

It came to me. "Danny. Danny McLintoch. How the hell are you doing?"

Danny had come into my shop a couple of years back to buy an anniversary gift for his wife, who'd just given birth to their first baby. He wanted something special, but was on a limited budget. I'd cut him a really good deal on a half eternity ring. He'd come back to the store to tell me how much his wife had loved it and it had made me feel good to know that I'd helped these two young people who were just starting out on the great adventure of family life. It didn't matter that I'd lost money on the ring.

A big grin split Danny's good natured face as he sauntered toward me. "For a minute there I thought you'd forgotten me."

I shook my head. "I never forget a customer."

That's actually a lie. I suffer from CRS, better known as 'can't remember shit.' I just got lucky with Danny.

"So how've you been? How's that beautiful wife of yours and your son. He must be what, two years old now?"

He nodded. "Wow, you do have a good memory. And, they're both good. Me, too. I'm working a second job here doing security to make some extra money. How about you?"

I shrugged. Danny frowned and proffered his pack of cigarettes. "What's up?"

I was tempted to take one, but shook my head. I'd quit smoking three weeks before Theresa had left and I damn well wasn't about to start again no matter what happened. I explained everything to Danny, finishing with the stolen tickets.

"I'm so sorry," Danny said when I'd finished. "That just sucks."

"Yep. It does."

"So, you're trying to get in so you can see if someone's sitting in your seats, right?" Danny was smarter than he looked, but then I knew that already.

I grinned and nodded.

He inclined his head toward a door behind the dumpsters.

"Back door," he explained. "Go through there and turn right. Keep going and it'll bring you out on the second level. Reckon you can find your way from there?"

I nodded. "Thanks Danny."

"No thanks needed. You did me a favor once and I reckon I'm just returning it. I'm happy to do it, too. But, if anyone asks, it wasn't me that let you in, OK?"

"OK."

Danny's directions were perfect and it wasn't long before I found myself inside the stadium. The game was in full swing now and, by the sound of it, the home team was winning. The crowd was roaring and singing and stamping. It felt like the whole building was moving.

I followed the wide corridor around until I came to the section I'd bought tickets for. I saw the cops right away. There were two on every section entrance. And they weren't hiding the fact they were there either. The people who'd stolen my tickets would have had to have been really dumb not to have seen the cops and just kept on walking right out of the place again. I was curious though, and I'd come this far, so I parted the curtain to the section and walked through. The noise hit me like a wall. I rocked back on my heels for a moment.

There were cops in here, too, patrolling the walkways between the seats and no doubt making some of the patrons more than a little nervous. I scanned the rows of seats. The ones I'd had tickets for were empty.

"What the hell are you doing here?" It was Detective Sergeant Gibson. "I thought we told you to leave this to us?"

"Yeah, you did," I laughed, but there was no humor in the sound. "And you did a real good job. This place is crawling with uniformed cops. No one in their right minds would have sat in those seats with cops everywhere."

"We're just doing our job," Rebecca Ward had somehow materialized on the other side of me. I hadn't even heard her.

I looked at her. I was taller than her, but only just. "Really? Because it looks to me like you're doing your very best to scare away the people that stole my tickets."

Despite the noise in the arena, people were starting to stare. Ward grabbed my elbow and tried to push me toward the exit. "Come on. Let's go."

It was an order and she was strong.

For a moment, I considered resisting, but what was the point? If the robbers had turned up for the game, they'd have been scared off by the heavy police presence long before they ever got near those seats.

I shook her hand from my arm. "Fuck you."

"Sergio."

I could hear her stomping down the passageway behind me, her footsteps echoing on the concrete. "Sergio. Stop."

I spun around. "Is that an order?"

Her honey-blonde hair was pulled back from her face in a ponytail. Her eyes looked tired. She sighed. "Look, we really are doing our best here, y'know? It's not easy catching a crew like this when we have nothing to go on."

"Your boss seems to think he has me to go on." I eyed her. "And, as long as you guys are focusing all your energies on finding evidence that I was involved, you'll never catch the real crooks."

She opened her mouth and then shut it again.

I shook my head slowly and smiled. Not that I was finding any of this remotely funny. "You can't even deny it. Fuck. Why won't you guys believe me?"

I took a deep breath, carefully enunciating each syllable of every word, "I had nothing to do with robbing my store."

I stopped, realizing that I was breathing hard and that I had moved closer to her. I was practically yelling into her face. I took a step back. "Look, I'll even take a lie detector test. Why would I volunteer to do that if I was involved?"

She held up her hands. "OK. I'll arrange for a lie detector test. I'll call you with the details of when and where. But you have to do something for me in return."

"What?" I could hear the belligerent tone in my voice, but didn't care. I was done playing nice with this lady.

"Leave the police work to us. Stop chasing round after missing hockey tickets and stop looking for that woman who took you home that night."

"Why? Have you found out who she is? She might be a lead. What if she was part of the gang that robbed my store and was supposed to keep me occupied while they—"

Not many women can make me stop talking with a single look. This one could.

"Listen Sergio, the crew that robbed your place was professional. Very professional. Crews like that don't leave anything to chance. Do you understand? They'd probably followed you for a while and had a pretty good idea of your routine. They almost certainly knew that if you were at a Rough Riders poker game, you weren't likely to be any trouble to them. They didn't need to hire some woman to take you home and make sure."

She put her hands on her hips and tilted her head to one side. She smiled and I was reminded how cute I thought her dimples were. "I'm sorry. I know you thought she was some kind of hot lead. But you must see that she's really not."

This time it was me who was lost for words. Damn. She was right. And I knew it. I'd been on a wild goose chase looking for that blonde chick, thinking that she might have had something to do with the robbery, but it had all been a waste of time.

Ward turned and walked away.

"She could still provide me with an alibi," I called after her.

"If you can find her, maybe. But, if she was as drunk as you were, she might not even remember who you are."

And I knew she was right. About everything.

CHAPTER FIVE

Ward called me about the lie detector test two days later. I was ecstatic as I headed down to the precinct house. I was sure this was the turning point. From here, everything would start to get better. The cops would finally believe I had nothing to do with the robbery, the insurance company would pay up, and I'd be able to get on with trying to rebuild my business and my life.

Ward and Gibson met me and escorted me into a small windowless room that was sparsely furnished with a table and two chairs. A large mirror covered one of the walls. Beside the table was the polygraph machine and beside the polygraph machine was a woman with graying hair pulled back into a bun. She was wearing a grey skirt and cardigan. Her spectacles hung on a chain around her neck.

"Mr. Pages, this is Linda DeFazio. She'll be conducting the polygraph test today. Linda, this is Sergio Pages."

I took a step forward and stuck out my hand. "Hi Linda. It's nice to meet you."

Linda DeFazio put her glasses on her nose. She looked me up and down, her eyes resting finally on my out-stretched hand.

She nodded her head curtly and indicated one of the chairs. "Mr. Pages, if you'd like to sit here, please?"

Embarrassed, I jammed my hands into my jeans pockets and sat in the chair.

Ward and Gibson left. I figured they'd gone to watch from behind the two-way mirror. Suddenly, I didn't feel so good. I was sweating hard.

"Mr. Pages, can you please lean forward in your chair and stretch your arms out in front of you?"

I did as she asked and felt her fix something around my chest. Then she placed straps on my fingers and a band, like a blood-pressure cuff, around my upper arm.

"OK. Are you ready?"

I nodded. I wanted to wipe the perspiration from my face, but didn't want to draw attention to the fact that I was sweating so much.

"Is your name Sergio Pages?"

I swallowed. "Yes. Yes it is."

"Just a 'yes' or 'no' will do, thank you, Mr. Pages."

Other simple questions followed.

"Do you live at 69 Acacia Avenue?"

"Yes."

"Do you own a jewelry store?"

"Yes." I was starting to get impatient.

"Do you intend to be completely truthful during this polygraph test today?"

The question was unexpected. The intonation and tone of her voice hadn't changed at all.

"Yes, of course I do."

She made a mark on the moving paper on the polygraph machine. I wondered what it meant.

"Were you involved in the robbery of your jewelry store?"

I took a deep breath. "No."

"Do you know anything about the robbery of your jewelry store?"

"No."

Again, she made a mark on the paper.

"Did you help to plan the robbery of your jewelry store?"

"No."

And so the questions continued. When she was finally done and had removed the straps, I felt exhausted but happy. I was sure the test would prove my innocence.

DeFazio studied the graphs for a moment and then tore the paper from the machine and stood up. "If you'll wait here, Mr. Pages, Detectives Gibson and Ward will be with you shortly."

In fact, it was quite a while before the door opened and Gibson and Ward walked into the room. Gibson sat down in the chair across the table from me. Ward stood beside him.

"So, do you believe me now?"

Gibson stared at his hands for a moment, unable or unwilling to look straight at me. Finally, he looked up. I didn't like what I saw in his mismatched eyes.

"The polygraph test did seem to suggest that you did not rob your store, Mr. Pages, but..."

He paused for a long moment before continuing. "It also showed that you might well know something about the robbery."

I shoved my chair back and jumped to my feet. "What the hell is that supposed to mean?"

"Sergio, sit down."

I shook my head. "No. You guys have been after me from the start. And you've read whatever you wanted to read into that damn lie detector test. What? Is it really too difficult for you to find the real thieves?"

Gibson examined his fingernails. "'The polygraph tells us what it tells us." He looked up at me. "Nothing more and nothing less. And the polygraph is telling us that you know something about the robbery of your store."

I dropped back into my seat, stretched out my legs and stared at the ceiling. This was a nightmare and it was getting worse. "You can keep me here all night, shine a light in my eyes, hit me with your billy clubs and do whatever the hell else you want to do, but I'm not going to tell you anything different. I did not have any fucking thing to do with the robbery at my store."

I felt, rather than saw, Ward and Gibson exchange a glance.

"What about your ex-wife?" It was Ward who finally spoke.

"What about my ex-wife?" I was tired. All I wanted to do was go home and pour myself a very large drink. I knew I was wasting my time and my breath with these cops.

"Do you think that she might have been involved in the robbery? After all, half of the store is hers. Maybe she wasn't willing to wait for her share?"

I laughed. "That's stupid. Have you even talked to Theresa?"

Ward nodded. "She wasn't very cooperative. Do you think she'd take a lie detector test, too?"

"Why? So you can read into it whatever you want, like you've done with me?" I shook my head. "No, I don't think so. And anyway, Theresa would be stupid to have the place robbed. With the store out of business, I'm not going to be able to pay her for her share. And she knows that, so why rob the place?"

I stood up. I'd had enough. "Can I go now? Or am I under arrest?"

"You're not under arrest." It seemed to me that Gibson said the words with a great deal of reluctance. I was waiting for him to say 'yet,' but he didn't. All he said was, "You can leave. Detective Ward will show you out."

I went straight to the nearest bar and ordered a beer and a shot of whiskey. And another. I ended up at O'Brien's. Not that I had any idea how I got there. I just woke up to find myself lying on the bar with Mo shaking me.

"Sergio, hon. It's time to go home. We gotta close the place up for the night."

She shook me again. "Serge. Where's your car, hon?"

I lifted my head. "What day is it?"

I heard her laugh and exchange some words with someone, but their voices faded as I fell back asleep again. They must have picked me up and put me in a cab because the next thing I remember I was outside my house and some pissed-off cab driver was yelling at me not to throw up in his car. He hauled me out and dumped me on my driveway.

That's where Serge Junior found me the next morning. He picked me up and helped me into bed, and that's pretty much where I stayed. I got up when I needed to use the bathroom or get another bottle of whiskey, but other than that, I hid under my covers. I was a mess and I knew it.

It's amazing how much a person can sleep when they're drunk and past caring. I didn't know if it was day or night and I didn't much care either.

The booze-soaked dreams ran one into another, impossible to tell where one ended and another began. Or what was a dream and what was conscious wakeful thought.

I dreamed I was a kid back in New York, standing in front of the old brownstone I grew up in. I could smell the delicious scent of freshly baked bread coming from the bakery on the corner and the not-so-delicious scent of urine that was a constant in the Bronx, especially on hot days. Or it was back then, anyway. We didn't have much money and life in that old brownstone was interesting, to say the least.

I dozed fitfully, passing between waking remembrances and drunken dreaming. I remembered sitting under my mom's coffee table late into the night watching TV as she did the ironing. Mom always was a night owl. Maybe that's where I get it from. She was also more than a little crazy. Mom watched The Tonight Show. dad watched adult comedy and lots and lots of news.

When I was maybe eight or nine years old, I went with my family to Jones Beach. I was standing alone in the surf when I felt something between my toes. I picked it up and saw it was a huge diamond solitaire ring. Even as a kid, I was sure it was worth a lot of money. My first thought was that I needed to return it to its owner. Actually, that wasn't quite my first thought. I still clearly remembered the day I'd gone across the street to a friend's house to play and had found a nickel in the living room. I'd pocketed it and when my dad found out about it, he'd beaten me so hard it still hurt. Then he made me return the coin. I definitely didn't want another ass kicking. So, I took the ring to the most important person on the beach: the 18-year-old lifeguard. I was so happy, I ran straight back to tell my dad. I figured he'd be so proud, but I was wrong. My dad called me an idiot and beat my ass. Doing the right thing sure was confusing for a kid. I guess I didn't learn my lesson though. A year or so later, I was walking along the street to the candy store. I didn't have any money for candy, but a fat little kid like me could always stare in the window and dream. As I walked, I saw a quarter fall out of a man's pocket. He was an Hasidic Jew, tall and dark with sideburns that curled down each side of his face. Without thinking, I picked up the coin and ran after him, tugging at his suit jacket to get his attention. When the man turned around, I handed him the quarter and explained how it had fallen out of his pocket. He took the coin and turned it over in his fingers before returning it to me.

"That was a good and honest thing you did, boy," he said. "You can keep the quarter as a reward and a reminder to always be honest in everything you do."

The dream slid away before I had the chance to take the coin to the candy store.

Consciousness returned and, for a moment, I wondered if Theresa leaving me and the store being robbed had all been a bad dream. I turned over and heard one of the empty bottles on the bed crash to the floor. And I knew it hadn't been a dream. Theresa really had divorced me, the store really had been cleaned out, and the cops and the insurance company really did think I had something to do with it all. Shit. I leaned over and grabbed the bottle beside the bed. It was empty.

"So, are you gonna spend the rest of your life in that bed or what?"

It was a woman's voice, but for a moment I couldn't place whose. And then, I put voice with face and name.

"Detective Ward. Who the hell let you in?"

I pushed myself up onto one elbow and stared through the gloom toward her. She was standing in the doorway, hands on hips. I saw the empty bottles on the floor and the mess of dirty clothes. Something told me that the room—and me too—didn't smell so good.

"I knocked on the door, but there was no answer despite the fact that your Hummer's in the driveway. I called the store and your son told me you were definitely here. He told me you hadn't been out of your bed in days. I tried the door and it was open."

She shrugged. "I thought something might've happened to you so I came in to make sure you were OK."

"Shit," I laughed but there was no humor in it. "I'll bet that's what you always say when you just walk into someone's place uninvited. What do you want? Come to arrest me for robbing my store, have you? Or do you want to search my place for the stolen jewelry?"

She turned in the doorway. "I'm going to make some coffee. You look like you could do with some."

She disappeared back into the kitchen and I could hear her opening cupboards, clinking china and filling the coffee machine with water. After a while, the enticing aroma of freshly-brewing coffee drifted into the room.

I rubbed my face with my hands and swung my legs out of bed. I figured if I didn't get up of my own accord, she was quite likely to come back in to the bedroom and drag me up.

I pulled on some jeans and a shirt, and shuffled into the kitchen. I looked a mess and I knew it, but I told myself that I didn't care. Only I did.

I dropped into a chair by the table and leaned my head back, wishing the light wasn't quite so bright.

She placed a mug of coffee on the table in front of me. "Cream? Milk? Sugar?"

I shook my head. "Black."

I eyed her as she sat down across the table from me. "So, are you gonna tell me what you're doing here?"

"I wanted to tell you not to worry about the results of the lie detector test."

"You want me not to worry about being told that while the lie detector test showed I didn't rob my store, it also showed that I might have had some knowledge of the robbery before the event."

I blew on my coffee to cool it. The smell made me realize how hungry I was. I wondered when I'd last eaten and realized I didn't know.

"Lie detector tests often produce uncertain results," Ward offered cautiously.

I finished the coffee, pushed back my chair and stood up. "And is that what Detective Gibson sent you here to tell me?"

She shook her head. "I'm off duty, Sergio. It's what I came here to tell you because I was worried about you. Gibson doesn't even know I'm here. And he probably wouldn't like it if he did know."

I opened a cupboard and pulled out a frying pan and then looked in the fridge for eggs and bacon. Sergio Junior had been shopping; the fridge was well stocked.

"You want some breakfast?"

She glanced at her watch and smiled. "It's two in the afternoon."

I shrugged. "How about a late lunch?"

I fried us some bacon and eggs with toast on the side. We had it with more coffee and, by the time I'd finished eating, I felt much better. Ward was enjoyable company and although we talked as we ate, we didn't mention the robbery or her work.

I watched her as she collected up the plates and rinsed them in the sink. "You know, the jewelry store is really all I've got. There's no way I would have had anything to do with the robbery, I've spent too much time and energy building that place up from nothing."

She sighed. "I know, Sergio, and I don't think you had anything to do with the robbery, but I also know how cops think. I know how Gibson thinks. And I can tell you that you're not doing yourself any favors by the things you're doing and the way you're behaving."

I frowned. "So I should just let it go?"

She shook her head. I liked the way her blond pony tail swung from side to side. It reminded me of the cheerleaders back in high school.

"No, you shouldn't just let it go. But you need to focus on what's important to you right now, and that's putting your business back together." She tilted her head and looked me critically up and down. "And, while you're at it, maybe you should do some work on putting yourself together or they'll start calling you Sergio 'The Mess' Pages."

"And how the hell am I supposed to do that when the insurance company won't pay out because the cops told them that I might have something to do with the robbery?"

She dried her hands on a towel and collected her purse. "You'll find a way, I know you will. You're one of life's resourceful people."

She left without saying goodbye.

I sat at the table for a long while thinking about what she'd said. She was right; I was resourceful and always had been. It went back to those early days in New York when relying on my wits often meant the difference between getting the crap beaten out of me by some tough kid or getting home in one piece with only my lunch money gone.

I remembered the times some tough kid I didn't know would tell me I owed him a quarter. If I didn't produce that quarter, I knew the guy would punch me out. I learned fast that it paid to stay out in the open where it was harder to get cornered and caught by those boys. I also learned fast how to take care of myself.

There was this one mean motherfucker called Butchy. He was an angry red-haired, freckled freak who seemed to love punching people more than anything else. I tried to stay out of his way most of all, but he still beat me up several times. I guess one day he must have messed with the wrong person because someone gave him a flying lesson off the fifth-floor roof of his apartment building. He was nine years old. At the time, I thought it was a hell of a good day.

And then, there was this sadistic little black kid called Stevie. He used to hang out with a crowd of white kids, but was only ever vicious when he had a gang to back him up. One day, the kids held me down and Stevie spit in my hair. I went home and my parents were furious. They took me right back downstairs and I called Stevie out. He wasn't used to a fair fight, but my parents made sure no one else got involved and I cleaned his clock. It had felt damn good, too.

It seemed there was always lots of fighting and yelling by kids and adults alike when I was growing up. One time a brawl broke out—I still don't know what it was about—but there were people fighting on all five floors of that old brownstone we lived in. And they were all members of the Pages family, too. It was wild.

Then there was the day two cops came to the door looking for an uncle of mine who ran numbers for the mob. I was just a little kid and, like lots of little kids, I thought cops were cool. My dad started screaming at them and asking them if they were there on official business. I was so scared, I went and hid under the table with my sister until he slammed the door in their faces. I found out much later that they were there because they'd not gotten their take money.

I thought that uncle of mine was pretty cool, too. I can still remember how I loved dressing up in a suit and fedora for church on Sundays. I looked like a junior version of him, a miniature mob man.

Things didn't get much quieter after we moved to Tampa. I was ten at the time and brought the street smarts I'd learned in the Bronx with me to Florida where I quickly became known as a trouble maker. I wasn't really. I just didn't take crap from anyone. When was 17, I had this bad-ass, souped-up 1968 Firebird. It had a 350 engine, a Holley four-barrel carburetor, a Muncie shifter and a 12-bolt positraction rear end with 50s on the back and 60s on the front. Damn, I loved that car. The clutch and pressure plate needed replacing, though, and the transmission would pop out of gear when I was cruising along in fourth, so I took it to a local mechanic. Three weeks and a lot of phone calls later, the mechanic, who was this burly, red-faced guy, finally finished the repairs.

When I went down to the garage to pick up the car and pay for it, the mechanic had this nasty attitude and was rude. But, he'd done the work, so I paid him and let it go.

Given the guy's attitude, I guess I shouldn't have been surprised when I found the car was still popping out of fourth. So, I took it back. The mechanic was not pleased to see me. One month later, my car was still in the shop and the mechanic wasn't returning my calls. That's when I asked my dad if he could help me out. My dad went up to the garage. When he got back, he told me the mechanic had started cursing him and calling him a spic. I thanked my dad for trying and told him I'd deal with things myself.

I went down to the shop and told the mechanic I was there to pick up my Firebird. He got nasty with me, but I just got in my car, which was parked in his garage, revved it to 3,000 RPM and dropped the clutch. I made so much smoke with those rear tires that I filled his garage.

Once his shop was belching smoke, I drove my car out of it. The mechanic came running after me, cursing.

I stopped the car and got out, yelling as I did so. "You want some of me, you big, fat motherfucker?"

If he thought he was going to pound my ass, he was wrong. As soon as he got close, I grabbed his neck in an arm lock and started hitting him with a billy club I kept under the seat of my car. I hit him several times before his employees managed to take the club off me. I figured that was my signal to get the hell out of there, so I hauled ass. I can still remember the sight of blood dripping from that mechanic's head

I hightailed it back home and called the police. I told them I was 17, had been attacked by an adult and had defended myself. A cop came out to my house and told me he was going go talk to the mechanic. When he returned, he asked me to step outside and I saw he had my billy club in his hand. He told me the club was a deadly weapon and that he should be taking me to jail for assault. Then he said that he'd been called out lots of times because that mechanic was always ripping off people in the neighborhood, and intimidating and threatening them when they wanted warranty work done. He told me I was a lucky young man because he'd convinced the mechanic that he was in more trouble than I was because I was a minor. The cop also told me that he'd be keeping the billy club. Then he headed back to his cruiser, but not before smiling at me and saying, "Good work, son."

I felt like a superhero that day.

I picked up my empty coffee mug and stacked the dishes in the dishwasher. Things had never really been easy for me. Yes, I'd been blessed with golden luck, but it was luck I'd made for myself with my own two hands. It was luck I'd worked hard for, but now it seemed like it had deserted me.

I knew Ward was right. I was being distracted by the robbery. What made me think I could catch the guys who did it? I might have felt like a superhero after I'd tangled with that mechanic, but what did I know about finding and catching criminals?

It was time for me to do what I did best—start making my own luck again.

CHAPTER SIX

My hunting place in the woods of Alabama isn't a great distance from my home outside of Tampa. And I like the drive. My Hummer eats up the miles and I get there in no time. I slow down and hide any open cans when I get to the state line though. It always seems like there are cops around the state line and I've been pulled over more than once. Managed to talk my way out of it more than once, too.

A sense of peace always flows over me when I turn off the highway and bump down the dirt track to my place. When Theresa and I bought it, it was a run-down shack on 80 acres of good hunting ground, and we worked hard to make it a real home away from home. It was rustic, but comfortable. And I was happy there. It was a haven for me, the place I went when I needed to really think. And, right now, I needed to think.

If I'd had the window down, I guess I might have smelled smoke or something before I turned the corner and saw the cabin, but it was a hot day and I had the air conditioner in the truck blasting out cold air and all the windows closed.

When I drove around the last corner in the track, I saw my place. It was half burned to the ground. I slammed on the brakes and the Hummer fishtailed to a halt. I stared, not believing my eyes. One entire corner of the cabin—the corner where the kitchen was—had been burned pretty much to the ground. I opened the car door and jumped down. The smell hit me: it was like old bonfires put out by rain.

Slowly, I crossed to the front stoop and unlocked the door. Not that I needed to; I could have walked through the burned-out wall easily enough. Inside, everything stank of smoke and there was soot everywhere. I looked at the devastation. I had no idea what had happened or how the fire had started, although from the scorched earth and trees outside, it looked like it had begun somewhere else and spread through the forest to my place. In fact, it looked like it had spread from Don McDonnal's place. He'd set brush fires before to clear out the undergrowth only to have them get out of control and burn things he hadn't intended. I figured that was what had probably happened here.

My hunting place in the woods was my last refuge. The one constant in my life that hadn't been touched by disaster. But now, even that was gone. And, as it was an unoccupied dwelling, I had no insurance.

It was my darkest and saddest moment. First, my wife, then the store and now my cabin in the woods.

Crying, I stumbled back to the Hummer, opened up the back, rummaged in the cooler for two cans of beer and popped one open. I took the cans to the huge boulder on the other side of my land and sat on it, surveying the wreckage of my cabin, which was visible on the far hill. I gulped my drink. Strange how cold beer can make everything a little better somehow.

I leaned back on the rock—it's as big as a bus, if not bigger—and closed my eyes against the late-afternoon Alabama sunshine.

I must have been tired because I dozed off for a while. I woke up hot and achy, and with beer dripping across the stone and down my leg. The liquid had attracted a couple of wasps and some ants, luckily not fire ants though. There were fire ants in the woods around my place and they were nasty sons of bitches.

I sat up and stretched as I watched the beer drip down the side of the stone and onto the scorched earth. There was a legend attached to this boulder. The person who owned the land and the shack that had stood here before I bought the place had told me about it.

All of the land hereabouts had once been home to Creek Indians, and the Native Americans that lived here thousands of years ago had believed that the boulder held magical powers and the ability to bring good fortune.

According to the legend, if a person stayed on the stone all night, recited holy verses and drank fire water, he'd find treasure. It was a cute story and the kids had always loved it.

Desperate and in need of more than a little good luck, I found myself wondering if there was any truth to the story. After all, many legends have a basis in fact.

I've always considered myself to be a lucky person, blessed in many ways. But now, it seemed like all my luck had walked out the door along with the weight I'd lost when I'd had the gastric-bypass surgery. I wondered if somehow, subconsciously, this was why I'd decided on the spur of the moment to come here. Maybe the boulder had been calling me. I laughed at the stupidity of what I was thinking and took another swig of beer. It was warm and decidedly flat. I poured what was left of it out onto the rock and watched it slowly evaporate.

Stupid though the thought of a magical boulder might be, I knew I was desperate enough to try anything. Besides, it might be fun and would definitely be a party. And I was always up for a party.

Firewater I had in the car. Whiskey. And lots of it, too. Wild Turkey 101. Good stuff. Sleeping out wasn't a problem for me either. I loved it and I knew there were sleeping bags in the cabin providing they hadn't been burned in the fire along with the kitchen. I'd just need to make sure I had plenty of wood to keep a fire going all night so the wild animals would stay away. Holy verses I didn't have.

I popped open another can of beer and thought about that for a while. And Vicky Mae Walker came to mind.

Vicky Mae, who lived right back at the end of the dirt road where it joined the highway, went to church every Sunday, regular as clockwork. A woman like that was sure to have a bible.

I tossed my now-empty can back into the cooler in the back of the Hummer and bumped slowly back along the dirt track toward the highway. I thought about heading out to Don McDonnal's place first and giving him a piece of my mind about the fire, but decided against it. And that really wasn't like me. When someone messed with me, I usually messed with them right back. But, for some reason, I felt in surprisingly good spirits despite my burned-out cabin. That could be fixed. In fact, all of a sudden, I had the strange sense that everything could be fixed. Maybe I just needed to believe.

Vicky Mae lived in a tidy little white clapboard, two-story house that was surrounded by large trees. It sat a little way back from the road, about 20 yards down from where it merged with the highway. Near enough to make for easy access, but far enough away to give the illusion of seclusion. She was a wonderfully sweet old-time Alabama woman with wrinkled sun-blackened skin. I figured she was at least 105 and always had a sense of time slowing right down whenever I was talking to her. She always went barefoot and I sometimes wondered if shoes had ever touched her feet; they were that wide and callused. She loved Jesus and had a little dog she called Dog. I'd given her a dog once, but the next trip out there I noticed it was gone. I figured a coyote probably ate it. Alabama is tough country.

I parked the Hummer and walked the plant-lined path to the green front door. Her garden was immaculate with neatly trimmed grass and tidy flower beds. She answered as soon as I knocked and I figured she must have been watching and seen me drive up.

"Sergio." She gave me a warm hug. "Nice to see you again. How's things? You want a nice glass of cold lemonade?"

I nodded my thanks and followed her into the cool kitchen at the back of the house. On the kitchen table was a small book and a piece of cloth with a large needle stuck in it.

She filled two tall glasses with her homemade lemonade and pushed one gently across the table toward me. I took a sip. Old Vicky Mae made the best damn lemonade I'd ever tasted. It was almost good enough to make me want to give up alcohol. Almost.

She picked up the piece of cloth from the table and started to sew. Her knuckles were bent with arthritis and I wondered how she managed to sew let alone thread the needle. "So, are you here for just a few days, Sergio? Or longer?"

"Just a couple of days, ma'am. I needed to get away and think."

"Your place OK?"

I shook my head and told her about the fire.

She tutted gently. "I didn't see nothing, but then your place is so far down the track you could murder a whole bunch of people down there and I'd never hear a thing."

I grinned. "Not planning on doing any murders." I sipped more lemonade. "Not yet, anyway."

She threw back her head and laughed until tears ran from her eyes. She dabbed at them with a little lace-edged, white handkerchief she pulled from her sleeve. "You have quite the sense of humor there, young man."

"Do you need anything from town, ma'am? I can pick stuff up for you, if you need groceries or anything?"

She perched her glasses back on her nose. "I'm fine thanks, but it was nice of you to ask."

I sipped my lemonade and watched her sew for a while. "Uh, Miz. Walker? I was wondering if I might be able to borrow a bible from you."

She pushed the small book across the table toward me. "Would that do?"

I opened the book and flipped through the pages, but couldn't find what I was looking for. "I was hoping to read from the Book of Psalms, ma'am, Psalm 23 to be precise. I can't find it in this one?"

There was silence for a moment as she continued to sew, pushing the needle in and out of the cloth with surprising dexterity. I had the sense of time stretching out. I saw she was embroidering a square of cloth with a biblical quote on it.

She saw me looking and held up the cloth. "It's Psalm 23, verse four. Strange, huh?"

She put the cloth down and got to her feet, disappearing into another room. When she returned, she was holding a large book, which she handed to me.

It was a bible. On the inside front cover was the Walker family tree. I stared first at the book and then at Vicky Mae.

She inclined her head toward the book. "Take a look."

I opened up the book and leafed through the heavy gilt-edged pages until I reach the book of Psalms. "Yea, though I walk through the valley of the shadow of death, I will fear no evil: for thou art with me; thy rod and thy staff they comfort me."

Vicky Mae smiled. "Funny how that book always seems to say the right thing at the right time, doesn't it?"

Back at my burned-out shack, I went into the big bedroom where I knew there were some sleeping bags and blankets. As I rummaged around, I realized that the majority of the house had actually been pretty much untouched by the fire. Everything smelled of smoke, but that was all. Only the kitchen had really been badly affected, but that had pretty much burned to the ground with only ashes and the occasional melted fork or spoon remaining. Maybe, I'd be able to fix the place up more easily than I thought. After all, I'd pretty much built it from scratch. The real bitch of it was that I had no insurance on the place because insurance companies would no longer insure unoccupied hunting cabins in the woods.

I took the oldest sleeping bag and blanket I could find, along with a couple of tattered cushions, and carried them out to the boulder. I brushed dirt and loose stones from the top and placed the bible on it. I was beginning to feel more than a little excited. Maybe it was childish to believe in such superstitious crap, but it was going to be a blast to try it out. With my place being so isolated, at least no one was likely to come along and see me. And that was some consolation.

The sun was dipping behind the trees and the drowsy peace of a warm summer's evening began to steal across the ground even though it was still early in the year. Even my burned-out cabin on the far hill looked better in the rosy light of the fading day. I stirred myself. If I was going to do this, I needed to prepare.

I crossed to the trees and started to pick up sticks of various sizes. I knew I'd need to keep a small fire going all night to make sure I wasn't bothered by any wild animals. There was plenty of kindling on the ground and I didn't have to walk far into the forest to collect all that I needed. I made two trips to the trees, each time returning with an armful of kindling, which I placed beside the large boulder, a safe distance from where I was planning to have the fire. After what had happened to my place, I wasn't about to take any chances with fire. By the time I'd built a small fire pit and laid and lit the fire, it was starting to get dark.

I opened the cooler I'd brought from the Hummer and cracked open a bottle of whiskey. I lay on my back on the boulder, smelling the wood smoke from the fire and toasting the stars as they slowly started to appear in the ever-darkening sky. This was probably my favorite time of the day, when the inky-blue darkness of night slowly ate the light of day and replaced it with the clean beauty of light from far-distant planets.

Silence descended along with the darkness, broken only by the crackle of the fire, the music of the Whip-Poor-Wills and a cacophony of yips from a distant pack of coyotes that was gathering for the evening hunt. It's funny how that sound always makes the hair stand on the back of my neck.

I took a deep breath, drinking it all in. Then I sat up and opened the bible. I had no plan, I just opened the book at a random page. It was Psalm 23 again. I felt my skin tingle as I read it all the way through and then continued to read random passages by the flickering firelight, drinking a whiskey toast to each one. Every now and then, I paused to put some more sticks on my little fire.

I'm not sure what time it was when I finally dozed off, but I awoke with a start to the sound of my cell phone. I sat upright quickly, too quickly. My head started to spin and the half-empty bottle of whiskey I'd been nursing in my sleep fell to the dirt joining the empty one that was already there. The fire had long since gone out.

I rummaged in my pockets for my phone and eventually found it. I flipped it open, trying to clear my throat as I did so.

"This is Sergio." I tried to sound normal.

"Sergio. My man." The loud and booming voice coming through the phone belonged to Herb Hitzig. Or Uncle Herb as I called him.

A salesman in his late 60s, Herb was a cornerstone of the jewelry industry and respected by everyone. He'd taken me under his wing when I was just starting out and treated me more like family than a business associate.

"Uncle Herb. Good to hear from you. What's up?"

"Absolutely nothing. I was sorry to hear about your store, my boy." He always called me that.

"Thanks, Uncle Herb. It really does fucking suck."

"Yep, sure does. Listen, I've spoken to eight wholesalers and we've all agreed to front you enough jewelry to restock your store. We'll give it to you free-of-charge for six months. You just pay us for what you sell. At the end of six months, you can return whatever you haven't sold. Does that sound OK to you?"

I was lost for words, and that didn't happen to me often. I'm one of those people who can not only talk the hind leg off a donkey, but also persuade it to go for a walk afterwards. But what Herb was suggesting was unheard of. Wholesalers in the jewelry industry don't do stuff like that. The value of the pieces is just too great. Everything had to be paid for upfront. Always.

Herb must have mistaken my silence for indecision. "Listen, my boy, you and me, we go way back. You've been buying from me for more than twenty years. I know you're honest and I know that you're good for whatever pieces you take. We wanna help. OK?"

Humbled wasn't the word for how I felt right then. "Thanks, Uncle Herb. I can't begin to tell you what this means to me."

His laugh was as deep and booming as his voice. "Good. Come by anytime and let me know what pieces you want. Take care, my boy."

The phone went dead.

The sun was rising up above the tree line, spreading fingers or warmth and light onto the ground. I looked at the bible on the boulder beside me and then at the bottles of whiskey. What Herb was offering was more than a lifeline, it was a miracle. I'd be able to reopen my store and start to make money. Without his offer, I would've had to have waited until I had the hundreds of thousands of dollars I'd need to buy jewelry to sell. This way, I'd be back on my feet in no time.

I almost couldn't take it all in. This was as big a piece of good fortune as the one that had gotten my jewelry store started in the first place.

My dad taught me to work hard, save for my future and put away as much money as possible for retirement. I'd started out with nothing and had worked damn hard to earn everything I had. I got started in the jewelry business when I was still in college, when I got a job as a salesman at a little jewelry kiosk at the local mall. It was a small place; Little Annie had been my boss there, but I worked long and hard and was their number one salesman within a month and a half.

One day, I noticed this guy hanging around the place watching me. I figured he was probably gay. After a couple of weeks, he finally approached me. I thought he was going to make a pass at me and I was all ready to tell him—quite politely—that I didn't play for that team and that I was a pitcher not a catcher. But, I was wrong. He introduced himself, told me his name was Joe and said he owned a small jewelry store and was interested in me running it for him. He said he'd been watching me and liked how I worked.

Joe's place wasn't much bigger than the kiosk, but after a while I persuaded him to open a real store. I made a deal with him. I told him that I'd build up his jewelry business and turn it into a multi-chain organization. In return, he had to promise I'd be his second-in-command. I never got it in writing, of course. Turns out, that was pretty stupid of me.

I kept my side of our bargain and soon the store was doing extremely well. That's when he met and married this woman, and the two of them decided they didn't need me anymore. They decided they were going to run the store themselves. So, I quit.

I was newlywed, unemployed and living in a run-down dump of a one-bedroom apartment with Theresa and our baby daughter, Jessica Nicole. Theresa said quitting was a dumb move. She was probably right.

Two weeks later the phone rang. It was a wholesaler I'd done business with when I'd worked at Joe's store. He told me he wanted me to open my own store. I laughed my ass off and explained to him that I didn't have a pot to piss in let alone the money to open a jewelry store. He told me he'd front me the jewelry. The only caveat was that I had to be able to return it or pay for it at a moment's notice. I knew this was a golden opportunity. My chance to make it big.

Twenty-five years later, Sergio's Jewelry is a landmark. It took a lot of hard work to get there, but it was worth every drop of blood and sweat and every tear.

I picked up the half empty bottle of whiskey, wiped the dirt off the neck and lifted it in a silent toast to the sun and the people who'd believed this place was magical. I took a large swig of the amber liquid and rolled it around my mouth for a moment, savoring the way it warmed everything, before swallowing it. Then I stood and ceremoniously emptied the bottle over the stone.

Perhaps there was something to that old legend after all. I'd certainly found my treasure: my luck. Sergio was back.

Despite my stadium-sized hangover, I drove straight home, stopping only for coffee—strong, black, no sugar—at the first open place I found on the highway.

The first thing I did when I got back to Tampa, after taking a shower and swallowing a handful of Advil for my pounding headache, was to head over to Herb's place. I wanted to thank him again for what he was doing. Then I headed to the store. I'd been there only a couple of times since the robbery and I knew that I'd let Sergio Junior down by allowing the robbery and everything else get me so depressed.

I had no idea when—or even if—the insurance company would settle my claim. I was on my own. But Herb had given me a way out. I was going to reopen my store. I'd even decided on when—Valentine's Day. It seemed apt. It's the second biggest occasion of the year in the jewelry business, too.

Sergio Junior was at the store when I got there. I gave him a hug.

"Sorry, Serge." I've never been afraid to admit to my kids when I fuck up. "I really messed up, didn't I?"

My son pulled a wry face and semi shrugged.

"I know I haven't been here to help you clean up or anything, or to even start thinking about how we're going to get this place open again. I've been too busy feeling sorry for myself and trying to figure out how I was going to find the bastards that robbed us. But all that's gonna change."

The store was still a complete mess. Sergio Junior had arranged for a company to come and pump out the water, but the place remained sopping wet and would take a while to dry out completely.

I set Sergio Junior to work finding an industrial cleaning company that would come and clean the place up and take away the mess, while I went into the back office. My laptop was gone, the desktop computer was shot, and I'd need some new safes. And a new security system. There was a lot to do.

Before I got started though I decided to go to the cell phone store next door and chat to Carl. I knew he had contacts in the computer industry and I was hoping he'd be able to recommend a good place that might be able to salvage some information from my desktop.

It was a warm afternoon and the sun warmed my head as I walked the short distance to Carl's store. Although it was nearly noon, the place was closed. I knocked on the door and waited, but there was no sound from within and no lights either. Just darkness and silence. This was weird. The store had been closed up like that the day after my store had been burglarized, too. Carl was funny, talkative guy, and I'd never known him miss a day's work.

I went back to my own place and stuck my head into the back office. Sergio Junior was sorting through the papers that were strewn across the floor. He was keeping those that were important—and not so totally waterlogged as to be unreadable—and trashing the rest.

"You seen Carl recently?"

He looked up, thinking, then shook his head. "Can't recall seeing him in weeks. In fact, I don't think I've seen him since this place got robbed. I don't even remember him coming by afterwards to see what had happened and damn near everyone else did."

Sergio Junior was right. We'd had a lot of people come by in the days and weeks following the robbery, and more than a few of them had been good old American rubberneckers. But, I didn't recall seeing Carl at all. Not once. And that was weird because Carl was, by his very nature, a considerate and generous kind of a guy and I was sure he'd have come by to see if he could help out in any way.

"Maybe he's sick?" Sergio Junior offered.

I shrugged and wrote a short note, which I went and shoved under the door to Carl's store.

Back in my own place, I decided to start with the desktop computer. I figured there was probably no way I'd ever get any data off the hard drives, but I wanted to try anyway. All the information I had about jewelry that had been in the store for repair was on those drives, as well as invoices and bills. Figuring out what had been stolen and how to replace it would be much easier if I could get even some of the information from those computers.

I found a large container and started to dump all of the various computer components and peripherals into it. Some of them dripped water as I lifted them from the still-soaking carpet. I know nothing about computers, but I figured that probably wasn't a good sign. It felt good to be doing something though.

I took everything I'd collected to a computer store only to be told that there was nothing they could do to get any data from the drives. I wasn't surprised. The thieves had been pros. They'd stolen the back-up disk on which I'd stored my inventory and destroyed all of my paper files so I wouldn't have any records that would enable the cops to identify any stolen jewelry that did resurface. They'd probably dumped the computer in the water deliberately to make sure any data on it was destroyed. Like I said, they were pros.

Of course, the guy in the computer place charged me a couple of hundred bucks that I couldn't afford before telling me the computer was useless. I trashed it. Not that I could afford to buy a new one. But, right then, that seemed like the least of my worries.

Over the next few days and weeks, I tried hard to keep my spirits up for my two sons, if not for myself. But it's tough when it seems like the whole world—and most of your family—is conspiring against you.

Despite the robbery and my run of bad luck, my mom, dad and sister still refused to talk to me. Hell, even my own daughter had abandoned me. For some reason, they all blamed me for the break-up with Theresa, probably because of some lies she'd told them about me. They all seemed to believe every word she said. I hadn't even had an invitation to see them at Christmas, but Theresa had. I guess it was obvious whose side my family was on. Stupid that it came to choosing sides in the first place though. I could have told them some truths about Theresa, I guess, but that's not the kind of person I am.

When it came to my two boys, Juan and Sergio Junior, though, things were different. They both still lived at home with me and knew the truth of what had happened between me and their mom. They'd been around to see a lot of it, and the fact they'd chosen to stay with me rather than going to live with her spoke volumes.

Days dragged into weeks and weeks into months. February 14th came and went. My dream of opening the store again for Valentine's Day was just that—a dream. I felt like I was no nearer to opening the store than I had been the day after it had been robbed. To make matters worse, if they could have been worse, when I went to the store on Valentine's day to carry on cleaning up, Theresa served me with divorce papers. It's pretty low to serve someone with divorce papers on Valentine's Day.

I was under so much stress that I almost totally forgot about the springtime Tallahassee Parade. Luckily, Richey called me the day before to remind me or I would have missed it altogether, and that would have made me sad.

The Rough Riders are known for drinking and flirting and having fun, but our teddy bear runs are important to us and we take them very seriously. I love teddy bear runs; they never fail to warm my heart and make me appreciate how fortunate I truly am.

This year, the Tallahassee Parade was a two-day event. On the first day, we loaded two big Greyhound-type buses for a full-day teddy-bear run. We visited several hospitals, a number of special-needs schools and some orphanages. It was the biggest run we'd ever done apart from our Christmas Eve event. We all checked our uniforms to make sure we didn't have any off-color badges on our suspenders. After all, we do represent soldiers and have been known to have badges showing scantily clad ladies. We also didn't drink at all beforehand.

We worked hard all day handing out thousands of beads and almost as many teddy bears. We'd finished at the last hospital and were just leaving when a nurse came up and told us there were a few very sick kids in the Intensive Care Unit and asked if we would visit them before leaving. My Rough Rider friends, Grant and Brian, and I grabbed some beads and teddy bears and followed the nurse.

As we were going up in the elevator to the ICU, the nurse warned us that there were some quarantine rooms on the floor, which were clearly marked. She said we could knock on the doors to these rooms and, if the family let us in, it was all right to enter.

Grant, Brian and I worked the whole floor, handing out beads and teddy bears and trying to cheer up the sick kids. It can be heartbreaking to see these beautiful children so ill and in pain, and we do what we can to make them smile and forget their troubles for a few short moments.

When we arrived at the last room, we saw it was a quarantine room. I knocked and the parents invited us in. They'd heard about the Rough Riders and our teddy bear runs. We gave their beautiful year-old baby a teddy bear and, as it was our last visit of the day, we also handed one to mom and dad. As we turned to leave, we found our way blocked by a tough-looking, hard-ass male nurse who was steaming mad.

"What are you doing in here?" He sounded flaming gay.

Although there were three of us in the room, he focused on me for some reason. He jabbed his fingers into my chest. "Can't you read? This is a quarantine room." Each word was punctuated by a jab.

I tried to explain what the nurse had told us about entering quarantine rooms, but he didn't want to listen.

"Get out of here, right now. All of you." He turned back to me as we tried to leave. "And you..." He jammed his fingers in my chest again. "You are not allowed in another room in this hospital. Do I make myself perfectly clear?"

"Good," I gave him a big smile. "Because we're going to Disney World."

The first thing we did when we left the room was to find a hand sanitizer and cover ourselves with antiseptic.

"Why the hell was that nurse picking on me?" I asked as I rubbed the antiseptic onto my hands.

Grant and Brian both broke out laughing. "Because he thought you were cute, man."

When we got back to our bus, our colonel, Bill Hogan, asked what had taken us so long. We were supposed to be going to Hooters for a party and to be presented with an award for our charitable works. The detour Brian, Grant and I had made at the hospital meant we were now running late, and the guys were keen to get going. Once a teddy-bear run is over, Rough Riders have to go for a serious debriefing, which means beer time.

Bill called mc to the back of the bus. Working hard to keep a straight face, he told me that because the problem at the hospital had held everyone up and made us late for the Hooters party, I wouldn't be allowed to talk to any ladies for the remainder of the trip. Instead, my companion for what was left of the Tallahassee Parade was to be a little blond doll they'd found in one of the bags of teddy bears.

So, there I sat at Hooters all evening with my little blond doll. I had a feeling that wasn't going to be the worst of it though. I reckoned I was going to be stuck with the nickname "quarantine" forever, as far as the Rough Riders were concerned anyway. I was right, too.

The parade was a welcome break from my worries and I felt stronger when I got home, maybe because seeing those sick kids always put my own problems into perspective.

When I got home from the parade, I finished cleaning up the store and taking away all the mess and garbage. I still needed to repair and replace the display cases that had been smashed, refurbish and redecorate the inside to the store, repair the roof where the robbers had broken in and replace my three safes before I could take Herb up on his offer to let me have new stock at no up-front cost. And, I had no money to do any of that. My credit cards and line of credit were maxed out, and the insurance company wasn't any closer to paying out on my policy.

I was stuck in a classic catch-22. I couldn't re-open the store without money and without re-opening the store I couldn't make any money to use to re-open the store.

I was beginning to think that Herb calling and offering to front me jewelry so I could re-open had just been fate's way of laughing at me. It was truly ironic. Thanks to Herb, I could stock the store, but I couldn't afford to get the store back into a condition where I could reopen and sell the jewelry.

I hadn't seen the cops in a few weeks. I didn't know if that was a good thing or a bad thing. I tried to tell myself it was a good thing, but I was taking some convincing. I decided to call Detective

Ward and find out what was going on. She didn't answer her phone when I called, so I left a message asking her to call me back. She didn't.

The following day I called again and told her I'd call every day until she talked to me. That afternoon, she came by the store just as I was closing up. She followed me into the office and sat down in the spare chair.

"So, Sergio. What's so important, huh?" I could tell she was a little pissed. Okay, more than a little.

I shrugged. "I was hoping you might be able to tell me what's going on. You know, with the investigation into the robbery? Did you ever find anything out from those cigarette butts or the milk carton?"

"Our investigations are proceeding."

"That's it? That's all I get? My store was robbed. The insurance company won't pay out on my policy without me being cleared by the police. Even if you cops do clear me, they still need an inventory, and you and I both know that the thieves destroyed any record of that. So, now I have the insurance company's forensic accountants trying to piece together my inventory from old receipts and bank records. And all you can tell me is that..." I did a fair imitation of her voice, "our investigations are proceeding?"

She got to her feet, planted both palms on the desk and glared into my face. "There's really not much more I can tell you. We're pursuing some lines of inquiry—"

"Like what?" I demanded. "What lines of inquiry?"

She shook her head, making her ponytail bounce. "I'm sorry, but I can't tell you."

"And what am I supposed to do in the meantime?" I glanced up at her. "Can you tell me that?"

"Let us do our job. We'll find out who did this and then you'll be in the clear and the insurance company will pay out."

"And how long is that likely to take?"

"How long is a piece of string? It takes as long as it takes. But I can assure you that we are working hard to solve this case."

"Yeah, right." I shook my head. "You still think I did it, don't you?"

She closed her eyes and exhaled. "It's a line of inquiry we have to follow. We have to eliminate all possibilities. Including that you might have somehow been involved."

"Fuck. And what about Carl?"

She frowned. "Carl?"

"The guy from the store next door."

"I don't understand, Sergio. Why should we be interested in the owner of the store next door?"

"Because no one's seen him since the day of the robbery."

I could see that I'd finally piqued her interest.

"Really? This isn't your idea of some kind of a joke?"

I shook my head.

She pulled a notebook and pen from her jacket pocket. "What's his full name?"

"Carl Brooker. He and I went to school together. He hangs out with this guy who's a drug dealer. Maybe he was in some kind of trouble or something and needed money so he set up the robbery at this place. Why else would he have disappeared?"

"You'd be surprised. There are a lot of reasons why people disappear. I'll check it out, OK? But only if you stop calling me and let me get on with doing my job. Deal?"

I grinned. "Deal. Wanna drink? I was just finishing up for the day."

She glanced at her watch. "Bit early for me, Sergio. Anyhow, now my evening's shot because I have to go check up on this Carl guy."

She eyed me. "See, that's what happens."

The next few days were real busy. The Rough Riders' St. Patrick's Day Parade had kind of snuck up on me. I love parades and normally the St. Patty's Day parade is the highlight of my year. I'm on the organizing committee and I spend weeks preparing and getting things ready. It's our parade, we organize it from start to finish, and out of all of the parades we attend, it's the best. It's always held in Ybor City, which is just northeast of downtown Tampa, and also where the Rough Riders have their headquarters.

Ybor is my favorite part of town. Historic and oozing character, it was founded in 1885 by a group of cigar manufacturers led by Vincente Martincz-Ybor, and its original inhabitants had been the Cuban and Spanish immigrants who'd come to work in the cigar factories. There were still a lot of cigar stores in Ybor City, although none of them sold Cuban cigars any more. There was also Elmer's, a run-down bar that made the greatest devilled crabs and the strongest drinks to wash them down with.

I was so excited that I drank hardly anything the night before. This was the Rough Riders' day and I was going to help make sure it was the best damn parade in Tampa. I also wanted to make sure I impressed Dave, who was in charge of the organizing committee. I was hoping he might consider me as his replacement when he stepped down. His would be big shoes to fill, but I figured I was up to the challenge

I definitely didn't want to be hung-over in the morning, though, because, this year, I was in charge of one of the four sections at the start of the parade route that had to be marked off to park the 135 floats taking part. That meant I had to mark the streets with lines and a number that corresponded to each individual float. I had to work it all out using the exact length of each float. I also had to add space for emergency vehicles and tow trucks. And, like I said before, I'm not so hot when it comes to numbers.

Organizing a parade is a little like choreographing a ballet, only instead of dancers there's floats—and the floats are being driven by guys that are usually pretty drunk by the time the parade starts. And, if one of those floats goes the wrong way, I was fucked because there's no room to turn it around. Trust me, it's not easy.

I love being in parades, it's kind of like being a rock star. There are literally thousands of cheering and screaming parade goers and hundreds of signs that say, "We love the Rough Riders." It makes me feel very proud. There are always lots of pretty girls, too, who are more than happy to ask for beads by lifting up their shirts and showing their breasts to the world. We have a

126

name for it when they do that; we say that they're letting the puppies breathe.

Despite the fact that I really like the ladies, I'm not into that kind of stuff at parades, though. For me, parades are about entertaining the kids and the old folks in the crowd. This St. Patrick's Day Parade was no exception.

It was a beautiful day and, despite more than one drunken float driver, the floats did their dance without a single misstep. I felt good about things and, once the parade began, I did my usual stuff. That is, I handed out my beads to the young kids in the crowd who were having a hard time snagging them from the older kids or the drunks. What makes me happiest, though, is giving my beads to someone who's handicapped or to an elderly person.

About half way around the parade route, I saw this sweet-looking old lady in a wheelchair. She was incredibly wrinkled, like a prune that had been double dried and then dried some more. The skin on her hands was papery and thin, and splotched with liver spots. Her face was soft and powdery and her eyes sparkled behind her spectacles. She must have been at least 90. She reminded me of my own grandma, who died more years ago than I can remember.

I fought my way through the crowd and gave her my finest and most expensive beads. And, of course, I also gave her the obligatory kiss on the cheek. Before I knew what was happening, she had grabbed me and stuck at least three inches of her tongue down my throat. It was disgusting. Dirty old grandma. I gagged and thought was going to throw up.

I staggered back through the crowd trying not to step on kids and babies as I wiped my tongue clean with the back of my hand. I couldn't get the taste of her spit out of my mouth. I grabbed my flask and took a shot of Wild Turkey to kill the germs and take away the revolting taste. The 101-proof alcohol helped get rid of the taste and the memory of the dirty old granny, and I refused to let the incident put a damper on the rest of the day. Life's an adventure.

The parade helped me forget about the mess my life was in, but not for long. A few weeks later, I was sitting at my desk in the back office trying to figure out where the hell I was going to find seventy grand to buy some new safes. I hadn't heard anything from Ward, but that seemed to be the way of things with the cops. They didn't seem to be in any kind of a hurry. And that just left me in limbo.

I gazed through the two-way mirror into the gloomy store and beyond to the road outside. It was pouring with rain again. April had brought with it a lot of hot Florida rain and the raindrops trickled down the glass. Like tears. Even the weather was depressed.

The phone rang. I looked at it, but let it ring. I hadn't been answering the phone much. I was trying to avoid having to talk to my customers who had lost jewelry in the burglary. They all had questions I couldn't answer. I felt bad because I knew I'd let my customers down, many of whom I'd known for years and loved like family.

Whenever the phone rang now, it made me feel sick to my stomach. I was sure this phone call would be just another customer wanting to talk about a piece of jewelry that had been in with me for repair and which I would be unable to ever return. I sighed.

Although talking to my customers made me feel physically sick, ignoring their phone calls was making me feel like a real heel. I might drink and I like to party, but I've also always tried to be honest and to treat people right. To treat them as I'd like to be treated. I believe in heaven and hell, and I trust in God and Jesus Christ.

I remembered old Vicky Mae Walker's bible and how I opened it up and leafed through the heavy gilt-edged pages until I reached the book of Psalms. "Yea, though I walk through the valley of the shadow of death, I shall fear no evil: for thou art with me; thy rod and thy staff they comfort me." And I felt comforted.

I knew I couldn't ignore the phone calls forever. The stolen jewelry was my responsibility. It had been in my care and it was up to me to replace it one way or another. I wasn't sure how or when, but I would replace every piece eventually.

I took a deep breath and picked up the phone. "Hi, this is Sergio's Jewelry. Sergio speaking."

I could hear the tiredness in my voice. I needed to sleep. For about six months.

"Is this Sergio Pages? Sergio, you don't know me, my name's Dave. I'm a friend of your cousin Terry's."

I squeezed the bridge of my nose with finger and thumb to concentrate my thoughts. "Uh, sure. Hi. What can I do for you, Dave?"

I heard a low chuckle. "Well, it might be more what I can do for you, Sergio. I'm a contractor and I'm building out the space where there used to be an old jewelry store. There are two honking great safes in here and the new tenant wants us to get rid of them fast. Terry told me about what happened at your place and I thought they might be of some use to you?"

I was wide awake now. "Wow, thanks for thinking of me, Dave. I was just sitting here wondering how the hell I was going to afford to buy two new safes. I sure as hell can't reopen my business without vaults to keep the jewelry in overnight. What make are they?"

He told me. I told him I liked what I heard.

130

"Cool." I could hear he was smiling. "Then here's the deal. I figure I can convince the landlords to sell the safes to you for two grand apiece. What do you reckon?"

What did I reckon? I was stunned and elated and lost for words, all at the same time. And, that didn't happen to me all that often. I had the gift of the gab, as my mom would say, and always had something to talk about, some yarn to spin. But, right then, I wasn't sure what to say. Those safes normally cost $35,000 each.

When I found my voice, I told Dave 'yes.' I'm not sure if I even remembered to thank him.

CHAPTER SEVEN

One thing I've found in life is that things are rarely as simple as they appear. That was the case with the safes. I waited to hear from Dave. Eventually he called. He told me the landlords had figured out the safes were worth far more than two grand.

"They've decided to take sealed bids," Dave reported. "And sell to the highest bidder."

"Shit."

"Yeah, I know," Dave agreed. "It sucks, huh?"

"Yeah," I agreed. "But maybe there's a way. Who's the landlord?"

Dave reeled off a name, address and phone number. I scribbled them down onto the pad of paper in front of me. "Thanks, Dave. Stay in touch. OK?"

"You got an idea, Serge?"

"Yeah." I grinned. "I sure do. I'm going to go talk to the landlord."

Turns out the landlord was a landlady. It took me a few days to fix up a time to meet her. I dressed in my best suit and left early to make sure I wasn't late. I have a bad habit of being late for things, and this was one occasion I wanted to be on time.

The weather was fine and traffic was light, and I arrived a good 20 minutes early. I rolled down the window and lit a cigar as I sat in the Hummer and thought about what I was going to say. It was a beautiful day. The birds were singing and the hot sun streamed in through the open window, warming the left side of my face.

I decided to tell her the truth. Everything. The weight loss. The divorce. The burglary. I reckoned I had nothing to lose. What was the worst she could say? No?

The landlady's office was on the top floor of an older building in Ybor City. I figured I'd go to Elmer's afterward and eat devilled crabs washed down with cold beer, and then maybe stop by the Rough Rider's headquarters. I hadn't been there for a while and it would be good to go see what was going on.

The landlady kept me waiting for 20 minutes. Her personal assistant was very apologetic. I grinned and told her it was OK. I hoped the landlady would feel bad about keeping me waiting, too.

Finally, the door opened and a fine-looking 50-something woman appeared. She held out her hand. "Mr. Pages? I am so sorry to have kept you waiting."

Her handshake was firm, her fingers soft and warm. No rings I noticed.

"Won't you come in?" She ushered me into her office. "Would you like something to drink? Tea or coffee, maybe?"

I shook my head. "No thank you, ma'am."

She closed the door, indicating a comfortable seat beside the window. She dropped into the seat in front of me and gracefully crossed one long leg over the other.

"So, Mr. Pages, what can I do for you?"

She was beautiful. Her face had just the right amount of makeup and was surrounded by perfectly styled chocolate-brown hair with just a few elegant streaks of grey.

I grinned at her. It was hard not to. "It's Sergio. Please. Call me Sergio. And I'm here about the safes. Dave told me about them."

She pushed a few strands of hair away from grey eyes that were watching me intently. "OK. Sergio. So, you're interested in those old safes. Did Dave tell you that we've decided to take sealed bids for them?"

I nodded and told her everything. I didn't embellish or try to hide anything. I told her about the weight-loss surgery and how tough it had been. Then I told her about Theresa leaving me the day before we were supposed to go to Europe to celebrate our 25th wedding anniversary. And I told her how I'd kept the two boys with me and had never asked for a single penny in support from her. I talked about how my mom and dad and daughter had abandoned me and sided with Theresa and then, as if that wasn't enough, I told her about the burglary. I kept my head down as I talked, not wanting to make eye contact in case she thought I was just another scam artist on the make. I told her how the thieves had destroyed all my records so the police would have a hard job tracing any of the stolen jewelry, and how the insurance company was refusing to pay out on my policy until their forensic accountants had sifted through everything and pieced together an inventory. I even told her that the police, despite me taking a lie-detector test, still thought I might have been involved in the robbery.

Finally, I looked up at her and found myself staring straight into her clear grey eyes. "I'm actually in a position to open the store again because one of my dealers trusts me enough to let me have stock without paying for it up front, but without safes I have no way of keeping the jewelry safe overnight, and that means I can't reopen. And, if I can't reopen, I can't earn any money. It's a vicious circle."

The entire time I'd been talking she hadn't said a word, asked a single question or made one comment. She gazed at me and, for a long moment, I felt like we were in some kind of a staring contest. She didn't blink. Then, she looked away out of the window at the street below, brushing her eyes with her fingers.

"I'll let you have the safes for $500 each providing you haul them away. Deal?"

I opened my mouth and shut it again. Then opened it again. "I can't begin to tell you—"

She waved a hand. "Don't. I spent a lot of years as a single mom. I understand. And I'm happy to be able to help, believe me."

I started to get out of my chair to hug her, but sank back again, instinctively knowing that this would not be an appropriate response.

"Thank you."

It was hardly enough considering how I'd just been offered two safes worth a total of $70,000 for $1,000, but it was all I could think of to say.

As I bounded down the stairs and out onto the street, it occurred to me that I'd now had two enormous strokes of luck, first Herb and now the safes. Perhaps that little ritual on the stone back at my hunting cabin really had worked. It had just taken a little time for the good fortune to start returning.

I pretty much ran all the way back to where I'd parked the Hummer. I was out of breath and sat in the driver's seat for a moment before lighting up the cigar. I figured I'd earned it. I wished it was Cuban.

I opened the window and enjoyed my smoke. Then, I made a few calls. First, I arranged to have the safes moved that very same day. I didn't want to risk the landlady or anyone else changing their minds. I also decided I was going to give Dave $500 for all his help. He deserved it.

I finished the cigar and walked back up to Elmer's. I sat at the bar and ordered two devilled crabs and a beer. The beer was cold and full of life, and tasted like nectar. The devilled crabs were the same as always—the best damn crabs in Florida. It had been quite a day, and it wasn't even lunchtime.

I decided not to go down to the Rough Riders' headquarters after my crabs. I wanted to be at the store when they brought in the safes. I called Sergio Junior on the drive back from Ybor City and told him about what had happened. I was so pumped. It was hard to keep to the speed limit. But, the last thing I needed now was a ticket. Apart from anything else, I couldn't afford the fine.

Back at the store, Sergio Junior and I worked quickly to clear a path so the movers could manhandle the safes into the back office. After that, we figured out where in the office the safes would have to go and made space for them.

The movers came a little before five. They made lifting those huge vaults look effortless, although the things must have weighed more than a couple of tones each.

They were good safes. Top of the line, John Tann, maximum burglary resistant TRTL 60x6s. They were not only very hard to pick, drill or cut open, but could also withstand a plasma welding and cutting torch like the one that had been used on my old vaults. No one was going to break into these babies in a hurry.

I felt good as I watched the vaults being maneuvered into the back office and settled into their new home. I gave the moving guys a handsome tip. They'd done a good job and hadn't damaged anything as they'd rolled those safes in through the store. Once they'd left, Sergio Junior and I sat and stared at our new possessions.

"Aren't they the most beautiful things you ever saw?" Sergio Junior asked quietly.

I grinned. "Yep, they sure are. And they only cost us five hundred bucks apiece and five hundred for Dave. Now, that's what I call a bargain."

I spun around on my chair and gave Sergio Junior a hard high five. "Serge, my son, we are back in business."

The next few weeks were busy as I tried to get the store ready to reopen. I needed to have the display cabinets repaired or replaced, and I also needed to buy new computers and get them set up. I'd been hoping to get some of my financial and other information off the old computers—especially the inventory of all of the jewelry I'd had in the store for repair—but they'd been too badly water damaged for that. So, I had to pay a lot of money I didn't have to buy new computers and the best inventory system in the industry. I also bought off-site data storage. Paying for all of that put my line of credit way over its limit, but I wanted to be sure that customers who'd misplaced their receipts would be protected if I was ever robbed again. I hated to think about being robbed again, but I had to.

May arrived and brought with it hot, sweltering weather that was more reminiscent of August. It was preferable to the rain we'd had in April though. I was still working to get the store into a condition where I could reopen, but some days it seemed like I took one step forward only to be pushed two steps back again. Every day brought new bills to be paid, and I had no money to pay them, but I somehow managed to avoid drowning in debt completely.

May also brought the cops back to the store. I was sitting in the back office juggling bills, trying to figure out which ones to pay and when, when I heard the alarm on the door chime, telling me someone had entered the store. I shoved back my chair and pushed though the swing doors to see Gibson and Ward.

Ward looked as cute as ever. Blonde hair pulled back into a ponytail and dark sunglasses covering her clear blue eyes. She pushed the glasses up onto her head and gave me a half smile. Gibson was poker faced. I wondered if he had any other expression. His sunglasses remained on his face despite the fact that it was gloomy in the store. I was trying to save on electricity and had no lights on. Some people probably thought I was turning into a cheapskate, but I'd worked out a three-year plan to get back on my feet financially and being frugal was a necessity.

"Mr. Pages."

"Detective Gibson. Detective Ward. I'd say that it's nice to see you, but I'm not so sure it is."

I rubbed my face with both my hands. Shit I was tired. "What can I do for you?"

Gibson finally took off his sunglasses. "We thought you might want to know that another jewelry store got hit a couple of nights ago. Not too far from here. The M.O. was the same as when your store was robbed. The guys were pros. They came in through the roof and used the same type of gear to cut open the safes. They also left water all over the place to stop things catching fire. We're pretty sure the job was pulled by the same crew that robbed your place."

I leaned back against the wall, suddenly needing some kind of support.

Without a word, Ward walked past me into the office and brought a chair back in with her. She placed it beside me and pretty much pushed me into it. I was glad to sit down.

I took a couple of breaths. "Does that mean you no longer think I had anything to do with the robbery here?"

Gibson got himself a chair and sat down facing me. Ward remained standing, hands shoved into jean pockets.

Gibson opened his mouth and then shut it again a couple of times. It was like he wasn't sure what to say, or else he knew what he had to say and didn't like having to say it.

"We think..." he paused as if choosing his words with care. "We think that the crew that robbed your store probably originates from Cuba.

They're based in Miami and after they rob a store, they export the stuff back to Cuba before anyone knows what's happening. That makes it much harder for us to trace it—or them. They can get top dollar for it in Cuba, too. We think the leader of the gang worked as a welder in the Cuban shipyards, which is why he's so good with a plasma torch."

I eyed him. "You didn't answer my question. Does that mean you no longer think I had anything to do with the robbery here?"

He put his sunglasses back on his face and got to his feet. "We think it unlikely that you're part of this crew or that you had anything to do with the robbery at your store."

He shrugged, "but it's still a possibility."

I grinned. I knew that was the best I was going to get from Detective Gibson. But it was OK. It was enough.

The idea for opening the store on my birthday— June 10th—started off as a joke. Someone, I'm not even sure who, asked what I wanted for my birthday. Without thinking, I said that all I wanted was my store back. I'm not certain when it turned from a joke into fully fledged plan, but it did and, like always, I was going to make it happen. Even if I had to work 24 hours a day, seven days a week. And I pretty much did. Once I set my mind to a thing, there's no stopping me.

Things got a little easier after the cops told me about the other robbery. Maybe it was coincidence or maybe fate just decided that she was tired of jerking me around, or maybe my little ceremony with the firewater up at my place in the woods really had brought my good luck back. Whatever it was, things finally started going my way again. I started to find myself believing as I hadn't been able to since Theresa had left that maybe, just maybe, my luck had returned.

Restocking the store, pricing everything and building the new computerized inventory took every moment of my time. I usually have around 10,000 pieces of jewelry in the shop at any one time and that's a lot of stuff to source, price and catalogue. I figured I'd have to open with a greatly reduced stock because there was no way Herb would be able to front me that amount of jewelry, but it was better than nothing. And, at least I'd have something to sell when I reopened.

No matter how much or how little stock I had, though, it was useless to open the store unless I could attract customers. We'd been closed for a long time now and I knew I'd have to not only let people know I was opening again, but also remind them about the robbery. The only way I knew of to do that effectively was with a TV commercial.

TV's great for business. Or it is for my business anyway. And I needed to do a lot of business in those first few days. The fact that I also love making commercials has nothing to do with it. My plan for life had always been for Theresa and me to build a successful jewelry business and raise our kids, and then for me to go into acting. Theresa leaving me, the store being robbed and my hunting place burning down hadn't been part of the plan though. I guess life has its own ideas and doesn't always take much account of the things we plan for ourselves. I'd always wanted to be an actor, but I guess there are hundreds of guys out there who want exactly the same thing. The difference between me and them was that I tend to make the things I want happen. Or I had done until my wife and my luck had both deserted me at the same time.

In the past, I'd always written and starred in my commercials, and I loved it. When I was planning my very first commercial, I decided I wanted to show that Sergio was an honest jeweler. I was at a loss for a good idea, but then I remembered the Hasidic Jew and the quarter that had fallen out of his pocket. I remembered how he'd told me I could keep the quarter as a reward and a reminder to always be honest in everything I did. That was the idea we used for the commercial. We just changed the quarter to a dollar to account for inflation.

I got the perfect idea for my first post-robbery commercial from Alcohol Paul, the owner of the LA Hangout. Paul's a live wire, adrenaline junkie who talks a million miles an hour. He'd once won the Flair contest in Las Vegas and was awesome at coming up with marketing ideas.

One night, after a long day in the store, I didn't feel like going home, so I went to the Hangout for a drink. The place was jumping, as usual, and the patio was packed. The backdrop of noise rose and fell, like the swell of the ocean, through the haze of cigarette smoke. The pool tables were crowded and two tough-looking bikers were close to getting into a fight over a game on one. That wasn't unusual. Onstage, the band was setting up.

I lit up the end of a cigar and drained the remains of my beer. I was trying to decide whether to have another when Paul dropped into the seat beside me.

"Sergio," he clapped me hard on the back. "How's it going?"

He was talking to me, but watching the two pool-playing bikers. Paul's eyes were always focused wherever the action was, just in case he needed to jump in and calm things down. And he often did. He was a big guy, standing 6'7" in his socks, and few people were stupid enough to mess with him.

He signaled to the barmaid, Jennifer, who placed another beer in front of me. "On the house, Serge."

I watched the barmaid walk away. She was hot, all tall and willowy body with fine auburn hair that reached nearly down to her tiny waist.

Despite his nickname, Paul didn't have a drink himself. In fact, I'd never seen him drink when he was working, but when he wasn't working he could drink the best of us under the table and still come back for more.

I drank and wiped foam from my mouth with the back of my hand. "Thanks. And things are OK. I'm opening the jewelry store again. Real soon."

Paul swung to face me. "That's great news."

I frowned. "It is, but I need to make sure everyone knows about it, otherwise I won't have any customers. Not much point in opening the store again if no one comes to buy anything."

"What're you thinking?"

"A TV commercial."

He nodded, his attention back with the bikers as one of them slammed the eight ball down onto the table.

"Hey, I've got an idea. How about you make your commercial like one of those old-time cops and robbers movies?" He rolled up his sleeves and slid off the bar stool. "You know, where the robber wears black-and-white striped clothes and carries a big bag marked swag over his shoulder."

I grinned. "And the cops hit people over the head with rubber truncheons?"

"That's it."

One of the bikers threw his cue to the floor and jumped toward his bearded opponent. Paul was between them before either could land a punch. I watched him effortlessly haul both men out the door, the crowd parting before him like he was Moses and they were the Red Sea. I knew the commercial would be perfect. It would be funny, but it would also make people remember that I'd been robbed and bring them back into the store.

On my way home, I stopped off at La Tropicana on 7th Avenue in Ybor City and picked up Cuban sandwiches and Plantain chips for me and the boys for supper. I was tired and didn't feel like cooking.

Cuban sandwiches are amazing and La Tropicana makes the best ones around. A loaf of soft Cuban bread split open and filled with mojo roast pork, sugar-cured ham, salami, Swiss cheese, pickles and mustard. The ingredients are layered onto the bread in traditional order: ham, pork, salami, cheese and pickle with the mustard spread only on the top slice of the sandwich. There's nothing quite like it and I can remember my mom making sandwiches like these when we lived in that old Brownstone in the Bronx.

It was a nice evening, warm but not too hot or humid. I opened a bottle of cold beer and took it and my sandwich out back where I sat and enjoyed the view down to the water. I was thinking about how the hell I was going to pay for the commercial. I'd been using the same company to make my TV commercials for a while and had a good business relationship with them. But, I didn't have enough money to pay for another commercial. In fact, I still owed them money from the last one they'd made for me. And, as good as my rapport with them was, I somehow didn't think that they'd want to wait to get paid or do it for free.

I sighed and decided to think about something else for a while. I saw the key lime tree was dead. That sucked because I love key limes. The rest of the yard was becoming a jungle. When I was on my feet again and had the store back in business, I'd have to spend some time and money on the house. It needed new siding and a new roof, too, but that was going to have to wait for a while.

The front door slammed and Sergio Junior came through the kitchen and out onto the back patio.

I pushed one of the sandwiches across the table toward him. "Help yourself."

"You want something to drink?"

I shook my head. He wandered back into the kitchen to fetch himself a drink. I heard the hiss of a can opening and knew what it was.

Sergio Junior loves coke. I was always trying to get him to drink diet coke, which has 150 fewer calories than a can of the regular stuff, but he never listened to me. But then, when do kids ever listen to their parents?

He sat at the table, picked up one of the sandwiches and started to unwrap it. He took a couple of big bites and washed them down with coke. "Good sandwich."

I grinned. He had so much food in his mouth, it was hard to hear what he was saying. "Original Cuban sandwiches come from Ybor City, son, everything else is just a sub."

He laughed so hard he started to choke. He coughed until tears ran down his face. I thumped him on the back. Hard. His coughing subsided. He took a gulp of coke and then another.

"Where's your bother?" I asked when he was able to talk again.

"I think he had football practice tonight." Sergio Junior gasped and coughed some more.

The memory of my youngest son reminding me about football practice before I headed off to work that morning came flooding back. It wasn't that I usually forgot things, just that I had a lot on my mind.

"You're right. He told me this morning. I forgot."

Sergio Junior eyed me. "You forget a lot of things, Dad."

I threw a chip at him. "Don't fuck with your dad. I have CRS."

"CRS?"

"Can't remember shit."

He laughed. "So, what's giving you CRS tonight?"

I sighed. "How to pay for the TV commercial announcing our grand re-opening."

Sergio Junior picked up the bag of plantain chips and poured some out on the paper that had wrapped his sandwich. "Do we really need a commercial? I mean, really? Why not wait until after we open, when we have some money coming in again. Money to pay for stuff."

I leaned back in my chair and thought about what he'd said. The sun was hanging low in the sky. It would be dark soon.

I shook my head. "We've been closed for a few months now and lots of people will have forgotten about Sergio's Jewelry Store. And about the robbery, too. No point in opening again if we don't get customers in to buy things. We need to tell them that we're re-opening. We need to remind them about what happened. People will come out because of the robbery. Trust me. I know."

Sergio Junior pulled a half smile. "Have to admit that you are usually right about that shit. How the fuck are we gonna find the money to make a commercial though?"

I hated his cursing. I thought it made him look ignorant and Sergio Junior was anything but ignorant. I nearly slapped him on the side of his head, but stopped myself. I wondered where he got his tendency to curse and figured it must have been from his mother.

"I'm working on it, son."

We sat in silence for a while, watching the sun slowly slide down behind the trees and sink into the lake. The orange sky burned on the gently rippling water. It was going to be a beautiful day tomorrow.

"We still owe them $17,000 from last year's commercials," Sergio Junior reminded me.

I shrugged. "I'll offer them a piece of jewelry as collateral. I don't have to pay Herb unless we sell his stuff, so why not? I'll give them a piece that's worth more than the cost of the new commercial and what we already owe them. I'll tell them that they can keep the jewelry and do whatever they want with it, if I don't pay them what I owe them plus interest within a certain length of time."

I figured it would take more than that. I was going to have to convince those guys that the world would be a darker place without Sergio in it. My spending with them was tiny compared to most of their other clients, so it was going to be a hard sell, but my luck was back. I could feel it and I was in fighting mood. I wasn't about to give up until I got what I wanted.

"What do you think?"

Sergio Junior laughed. "It might just work, Dad. Someone's gonna have to persuade them to go along with the idea though. But then, you're the most persuasive person I know."

"I couldn't persuade your mom not to leave us," I reminded him drily.

"Yeah well, mom has some issues she needs to deal with. It wasn't your fault."

I shrugged and pulled off my shirt. It was getting hotter as the night grew darker.

"Dad, mom never appreciated what she had with you. She blames you for stuff because she doesn't want to admit the truth," Sergio Junior's voice was low and hard. "No one saw the way mom could be and the way she sometimes treated you, except us. It was like she was two different people. There was the person she was with everyone else and the person she was when it was just us."

There was another silence broken only by the singing of the blue jays and mocking birds. They were enjoying the unseasonably warm weather.

I heard the back door slam. My youngest son, Juan, had returned from football practice. I called to him that we were out back and there was a sandwich for him if he wanted it. He came through the kitchen door in his sweaty football gear and dropped into the spare chair with a grunt. His face was red and sticky. He peeled off his 'Property of Gaither High School' shirt and unwrapped the third sandwich.

Juan made me and his brother look tiny. He was tall, dark and a 295 pound monster of an offensive lineman. He ate like one, too, and a starving one at that.

Sergio Junior pushed what remained of the plantain chips across the table to his brother and faced me. "So? What about the commercial?"

I grinned. "You know me, son, I'm gonna make it happen. You see if I don't."

I managed to set up a meeting for the next afternoon with Brian and Joe at the video production house that made the TV commercials for my store. I appreciated that they'd managed to fit me in at such short notice and didn't mind having to wait while they finished up their meeting with another client. Their offices were in an industrial building. Lots of concrete and not much greenery. The front office was all glass and chrome. Modern and shiny; the walls covered with large modern-art canvasses. There were no windows, but then there wasn't much outside to look at except concrete and parking lot.

While I waited, I flirted with the receptionist. Marcie was 40-something with a nice cleavage and dimples. She was cute like a little girl, but had a sharp and sarcastic tongue. My kind of combination. And she had this laugh that was infectious. It was hard not to laugh along with her.

"So," I leaned my elbows on the reception desk and gazed into her big grey eyes. "What might a lady like you say if a guy like me asked her out?"

Marcie giggled. "I think she'd say yes. Why? Do you think a guy like you is gonna ask a girl like me out?"

I liked her answer. "How about tomorrow night? We could go dancing. You like to dance?"

She jumped as the door to the conference room started to open. She adjusted her blouse and straightened up in her seat. "I certainly do."

"Tomorrow night?" I asked, voice low.

She tore a sheet from her notepad and scribbled something on it. "That's where I live and my phone number."

I picked up the paper and folded it into my wallet. "I'll pick you up at eight."

"Sergio." Joe crossed toward me, his hand outstretched. "It's good to see you. How's everything?"

I took his hand and shook it. "Not bad, thanks, Joe." I shot a quick glance at Marcie and winked. She blushed. "In fact, things are pretty damn good."

He grinned. "Good. Come into the conference room and let's talk. You want coffee or tea or water or something? Beer perhaps?"

"Coffee would be great, thanks."

Joe told Marcie to bring coffee for everyone as he led the way into the conference room. Like the rest of the offices, the conference room was modern, expensively furnished and windowless. It still seemed somehow light and airy though, as if there was sunlight streaming in from somewhere.

Joe indicated a chair and sat down beside me. Brian came in and pulled the door shut behind him. He shook my hand and dropped heavily into a chair across the polished oak table.

Marcie came in with a pot of coffee, cream, sugar, cups and saucers, and spoons all nicely arranged on a tray. There was also a plate of chocolate chip cookies. She placed the tray on the table in front of Brian and left.

Brian grinned. "Chocolate chip cookies, my favorites."

Joe picked up the coffee pot. "Shall I be mother?"

Brian took a cookie. "Sure. Why not."

"Cream and sugar, Sergio?" Joe talked as he poured.

I shook my head. "Black, thanks."

"So Sergio. To what do we owe the pleasure of this visit? Do you need another commercial or something?" Brian had been born and raised in the U.K. and still had an accent that reminded me of how the Queen of England talked when she was on TV. He even did that thing with his little finger when he picked up a cup.

"Or maybe you've come to pay us what you owe us?" Joe added with a grin.

I took the cup of coffee he handed me and placed it carefully on a coaster. I'd thought a lot about how to approach Brian and Joe, but now I decided to just tell the truth. My luck was changing, I could feel it. After all, hadn't I just scored a date with the beautiful Marcie? The truth had worked when I'd been talking to the woman about the safes, too. I was on a roll.

Nikki Sinclair

I looked directly at Joe and then at Brian. I wanted them to know I was serious.

"I'm re-opening the store and I need a commercial, but I've no money to pay you. At the moment, anyway. I'm maxed out on all my credit cards and my line of credit. I can't borrow another dime." I held Brian's gaze. "We've done a lot of business together over the years and you guys are the best. And, right now, I need the best. I need a great commercial that'll bring people out to the store. Once they get there, they'll buy something. I guarantee it."

Joe spooned sugar into his coffee and stirred slowly. "So, you want us to do the commercial pro bono? For free? Or just not bill you for a while and hope you can pay us when we do?"

"You guys need to make a living, just like I do. I know that. I have a proposition for you."

Brian and Joe shared a glance. Both laughed.

"Well now, you know how much I do love a good proposition," Brian was still laughing. "What're you suggesting, Serge?"

"One of my suppliers has given me jewelry so that I can restock my store for the re-opening. The deal is that I'll pay him for what I sell or return what I don't sell. He's a great guy and a real lifesaver. It's strictly cash-on-delivery for jewelry in my business, and this guy is going out on a limb for me."

157

I drank some coffee. It scalded my mouth.

Brian steepled his fingers as he and Joe waited patiently for me to speak again.

"I'll give you a piece of jewelry that's worth far more than the cost of the commercial as collateral. If, by the time I get your invoice, I can pay you, I will and you'll return the jewelry. But, if things go belly up and I can't afford to pay you, then you can keep the jewelry."

I looked from Brian to Joe and back again. "What do you think? Can you help me out?"

"We don't need the jewelry as collateral, Sergio." It was Brian who spoke, but Joe was nodding his agreement. "You're a good guy and we trust you. We know you'll pay us for the commercial sooner or later. That's just the kind of person you are. Anyhow, what it costs to shoot one of your commercials is peanuts compared to what most of our clients spend."

"When do you need this commercial?" Joe opened his iMac and checked the calendar. "We're pretty busy, but I'm sure we can squeeze you in somehow."

I felt like jumping up and hugging them both. "Thank you, guys, you're the best. I owe you. If there's ever anything you need. Anything. You let me know, OK?"

Joe clapped me on the back. Hard. "If we were in trouble and needed help, I know you'd be the first in line. Do you have a script?"

I quickly told them the idea I had for the commercial.

Brian chuckled. "I love it."

"Let's make it kind of like the Keystone Cops." They spoke in unison. They did that a lot. It used to unnerve me when I first met them, but I was used to it now.

"Yeah," breathed Joe, gesticulating wildly. "The robber can be dressed in the classic black and white stripes with a big bag over his shoulder. It'll be great. And we can show you with your cut-open safes. It's gonna be way cool."

Before I knew it, the three of us has sketched out a rough draft of a script and also organized some time to shoot the commercial. Brian and Joe weren't kidding when they said their schedule was full, but they made some time for me. Like Herb, they were putting themselves out for me. More than that, they were trusting me to make good and repay their faith in me. And I was determined to do just that.

I pretty much floated out of Joe and Brian's office. I'd scored a date with Marcie and my commercial was going to be made, and in plenty of time for my planned grand re-opening, too. Life

was pretty good. I figured I was a lucky man
indeed.

CHAPTER EIGHT

When I got the letter from the insurance company a week or so later, I was scared to open it. If they'd decided to reject my claim, it was all over for me. I was bankrupt, owed more money to more people than I ever thought possible and was counting on the insurance money to be able to start paying off some of my debts.

I carried the envelope into the kitchen and laid it on the table. Then, I made a pot of coffee, poured myself a mug and sat down.

The door into the kitchen swung open with a crash and Juan appeared, tousled and sleepy.

"Dude, can't you do anything quietly?" I grumbled.

Juan grinned. "Someone's cranky this morning."

He nodded his head at the unopened letter on the table in front of me. "What's that?"

I picked up the envelope and turned it over in my hands trying to feel if good news or bad was inside. "Letter from the insurance company."

Juan frowned. "And you haven't opened it because...?"

"Might be bad news."

Juan laughed. His laugh was as big as he was. "You can't change what's in it by not opening it, Dad."

He was right, of course. I ripped open the envelope and pulled out the letter that was inside. I unfolded it. A check was attached to the bottom.

"See, Dad," Juan gloated. "Nothing to worry about at all."

I leaned over to give him a half-hearted smack on the side of his head, but he skipped out of arm's reach. "Gotta go to school. See ya later. Don't forget I have football practice tonight and there's a game Saturday."

The front door slammed and he was gone.

I grinned. Smart-ass kid.

The check the insurance company had sent was a partial payment of what they owed me. It wasn't much, but it would take the financial heat off—temporarily anyway.

I spent the next week juggling money and making deals during the day, and playing poker and partying at night. I was in my element.

It was a huge relief to be able to settle some of my outstanding bills. I hate owing people money. I was moving money around though, robbing Peter to pay Paul and then hoping I'd have enough money to pay Peter what I owed him when the time came. Voodoo economics, I called it.

I'd like to be able to say that everything got easier after that and that the grand re-opening went off without a hitch. It wasn't quite that simple, but I'd be lying if I said that things didn't get at least a little bit easier.

Now that I had the new vaults in place and a new security system installed, I decided it was time to bring the jewelry that hadn't been stolen back to the store. Since the robbery, the jewelry had been locked up in my safety deposit box at the bank. Although the thieves had taken just about everything and damaged most of what they'd left behind, at least they'd left me something.

It felt good to bring the jewelry back to the store. Kind of like a homecoming or something. I almost felt like we should have had cake. I could see by the look on Sergio Junior's face that he thought I'd gone slightly crazy. But, I loved that store like a child and I loved the jewelry, too. It spoke to me. One day, if he worked in the store for long enough, I knew it would speak to my son, too.

Not long after the jewelry's homecoming, I spent a couple of days with Joe and Brian, shooting the TV commercial. As always, I had a blast. I loved taping those commercials pretty much more than anything else.

With the commercial in the can, I booked airtime with my local cable networks for the grand re-opening. Every day, I getting a little closer to being ready. It was a good feeling.

I also had a bunch of flyers printed up. I was going to distribute them to all my current and past customers. I'd had the printer take a still from the commercial for the flyer and it looked pretty cool. Definitely very Keystone Cops.

I was exhausted from all the work, but more happy than I could remember being for a long time. One good thing about hard work, it takes your mind off all the other crap in your life.

I'd been working so hard and everything was so close to being ready that I decided to go out and celebrate. I started with a couple of drinks in the bar across the plaza. I ordered a whiskey from Mick and brought him up to date with what was happening at the store. He told me to give him a couple of flyers about the re-opening and said he'd put them up in the bar. It was a good idea, and one I'd not thought of myself. I ran back to the store and picked up a pile of flyers. If I was going to celebrate, I might as well advertise the re-opening of Sergio's Jewelry Store at the same time.

After my drinks at Mick's place, I took a cab and did a few of what I call hit and runs at my favorite watering holes. A hit and run is stopping by a bar, having a drink and then leaving. At each stop, I had a drink or maybe two and left a few flyers. Everyone seemed glad to hear the store was re-opening and they all promised to come. I hoped they'd all buy something, too. I needed to make a lot of sales and fast if I was going to start repaying my debts and getting back to where I'd been before the robbery. I was determined to be debt free within a year. Apart from the half a million I owed Theresa, of course, for her share of the house and the store. I had five years to pay her, though, and I wasn't about to give her a single penny ahead of time.

Being debt free within a year was a tall order, but I'd never been afraid of tough challenges. I liked them. It made me feel good to do stuff that other people thought was impossible.

I met Cyndi at Whisky Joes.

Whisky Joes is a great place to go if you want to get drunk by the water. And, that evening, after handing out all of those flyers, I wanted to get drunk by the water.

Cyndi was slight, but she had a laugh that was three times her size and could probably blow a house down from a thousand paces. She was sitting at the bar when I came in. Almost without thinking, I walked right up to her.

"It's cliché, I know," I grinned at her. "But, what's a nice girl like you doing in a place like this?"

She narrowed her eyes and looked me up and down for a long moment. Then, she burst out laughing. She had the cutest laugh lines.

"Gotta hand it to you, that's the best line I've heard all night." She held out her hand. "I'm Cyndi. And you are?"

I took her hand and kissed it lightly. "Sergio. Can I buy you a drink?"

She held up a bottle of Corona. "Thanks."

I ordered two beers from the barman and handed one of them to Cyndi when they arrived.

I held up my bottle and tapped it against hers. "Here's to a fun night."

She nodded. "I like the sound of that."

We found a table on the patio, which is right on the bay, and drank beer as we watched the sun go down. Then we drank more beer and ate fish tacos as we watched the moon rise. She told me about her two children and her two ex-husbands. I told her how I'd lost so much weight, how my wife had become my ex-wife and how my store had been robbed only a few short months before. When I told her about the store, she leaned forward, a wide grin showing a mouthful of slightly crooked teeth on her beautiful face. I thought those teeth were the cutest.

"I knew I'd seen you before. You do those television commercials for Sergio's Jewelry. That's too funny. I've seen you on TV."

She emptied her bottle of beer and giggled. "I've never met a TV star before."

"And, I've never been called a TV star before." I started to signal the waiter for another beer, but Cyndi placed her hand over mine.

"Wanna come back to my place?" she whispered.

"Now, that's not an invitation I'm ever likely to turn down. But, what about your kids?"

She grinned. "With their dad for the night."

That settled it.

By the time I got home the next morning, Juan had already left for school and Sergio Junior had gone to the store. It was June 9th and it was going to be a busy day, but we were pretty much all ready for the grand opening the next day and I knew Sergio Junior would be able to manage without me for an hour or two.

I brewed a pot of coffee, poured some into a large mug and took it out to the back porch. I sat in one of the chairs beside the pool and lounged back, enjoying the cool of the early morning. It was going to be another swelteringly hot day.

When Theresa had first left, Sergio Junior had asked me if I'd ever get married again. I didn't even have to think before answering 'yes.' I'd been married for so long, I wasn't sure I knew how to be single. Now, though, I was starting to meet so many beautiful ladies and beginning to think that maybe it would be fun to just play around for a while without being tied down to any one woman in particular. Life was pretty damn good. And, maybe life as a single guy wasn't so bad after all.

I finished my coffee and went inside to take a shower. Then, I headed to the store. On the way, I stopped off to pick up the new roadside banners I'd ordered that announced Sergio's Jewelers was open for business once more.

It was after eleven when I finally arrived at the store. Sergio Junior was in the office entering jewelry items into the inventory. There was no way we'd get everything inventoried by the time we opened, but we needed to have as much done as we could. The rest would have to wait until after we'd reopened.

Part of the problem after the robbery was that I hadn't had a complete inventory of everything that had been in the store, so it was hard to know exactly what had been stolen, especially when it came to jewelry that had been in for repair.

I'd finally managed to put together what I thought was a comprehensive list of what had been in for repair and was in the process of getting valuations based on my customers' descriptions of their pieces. At least then I could give them a piece of Herb's jewelry as a replacement because I had no way of compensating them financially. I'd have to pay Herb later.

If my insurance company made a full pay-out that covered everything that had been stolen—and that was a pretty big if—I'd be reimbursed for those pieces, but right now the important thing was to compensate my customers. It wasn't their fault their jewelry had been stolen. I was determined to get the store open again and earn enough money to pay those people who'd trusted me with their jewelry, with the insurance company's help or without it.

I joined Sergio Junior in the back office and we sat in silence for a while, entering jewelry into the computerized inventory system. Once entered, it would be easy for me to know what we'd sold, when we'd sold it and what I needed to reorder.

Like any father and son, Sergio Junior and I had our ups and downs, but he was a good kid with a heart of gold and I liked working with him.

At lunchtime, we went to the bar across the plaza and had beer and sandwiches. Afterward, I sent him home. I figured that the next day—the day of our grand re-opening—and, hopefully, the days and weeks to come, were going to be busy and it would be good for him to have the afternoon to relax.

I was shutting down the computers and locking away the jewelry when I heard a knock on the door. I glanced at my watch. It was after three p.m.

I put the remainder of the jewelry into the safe and swung the door shut, checking to make sure it was locked before I headed into the store to see who was knocking. It was Detective Ward.

I grinned as I unlocked the door and ushered her inside. "Detective Ward. What can I do for you?"

She glanced around the store. I'd noticed before that she had a habit of doing that. It was like she was taking in her surroundings and making sure nothing was out of place before getting down to business.

She motioned with her arm toward the big banners I'd put out by the main road telling people that Sergio's Jewelers was having a grand re-opening party the next day. "I saw your banners and reckoned I'd drop in and see how you're doing."

She pushed her sunglasses up onto the top of her head. "So, you're re-opening?"

"Yep. I finally got some money from the insurance company. And, some friends helped out with new safes and with jewelry to stock the store. I'm so pumped, tomorrow is going to be totally awesome. There's gonna be beer and food. It's gonna be a big party. You should come."

The dimples returned to her cheeks. Did I mention I'm a sucker for dimples?

"I'm glad. You deserve some good luck for a change. I hope tomorrow's a big success for you."

"Any news about the people who robbed this place?" I asked the question more out of habit than because I honestly expected the cops to have made any progress.

She shook her head and shrugged. "Sorry. They're a professional crew. It's gonna be real hard to get them. The only chance we have is if we catch them at it."

She brightened. "We did find your missing neighbor though."

I frowned.

"The owner of the cell phone store next to yours? Carl?" she clarified by way of explanation. "He turned up dead. They found his body way up in the woods. Coroner ruled it a hunting accident."

"So, you're telling me he shot himself? And, that's why he suddenly disappeared?"

She nodded. "Accidents do happen, you know."

I pulled a face. "Yeah, they do, but the chances of being shot by your own rifle when you're out hunting are almost non-existent. It seems pretty strange to me."

She looked me steadily in the eye. "Jeeze, you see conspiracies in everything. Let it go, Sergio, accept it was just an accident. And, don't tell Gibson that I told you about Carl or he'll be pissed with me."

I grinned. "I won't, but only if you come have a drink with me to celebrate my grand re-opening. And it's my birthday tomorrow, too. What do you say?"

She opened her mouth.

"If you say 'no,' I'll tell Gibson what you told me about Carl."

She shut her mouth again, the hint of a smile pulling at one corner of it. "That's blackmail, Mr. Pages. And I'm a police officer."

"An off-duty police officer," I pointed out.

"How do you know I'm off duty?"

I shrugged. "Lucky guess. Now, how about that drink?"

She threw her head back and laughed. "OK, you win. But just one."

We walked across the plaza to Mick's place and sat at a small table in the corner. I usually like to sit at the bar, but right now I was more interested in having uninterrupted time with Rebecca Ward. She ordered a Stella Artois beer and I joined her. When the drinks arrived, they were cold and refreshing. Perfect for a hot Florida day.

I placcd my glass on the table, wiping beer foam from my top lip. "So, tell me about yourself. After all, you probably know everything about me."

She eyed me. "Not everything, I'm sure."

"Well, certainly more than I know about you," I pointed out. "That's for definite."

She shrugged and drank some beer. "Not much to tell. I work. I go home. I feed Eric. I sleep. I go back to work again."

"Eric? He your boyfriend?" The thought of her having a boyfriend bothered me.

She laughed. "My dog. He's good company though. And he never complains when I kick him off the bed at night."

"What about your social life?"

She drained her beer. "I'm a cop. I don't have a social life. I go out for beer with the guys from work sometimes, but that's about it."

I signaled to Mick for another round of beers. I expected Rebecca to object, but she didn't.

"That doesn't sound like a lot of fun."

"It's OK. It's tough to meet people when you work odd hours, and then being on-call makes it harder. I make arrangements to go out with friends or whatever and something comes up and I'll get called out. People kind of get pissed off when they keep getting stood up all the time."

"I wouldn't mind."

"That's what they all say," she shrugged. "To start with. And anyway, I never mix business with pleasure."

"And I'm strictly business?"

"Yep." She finished her beer and stood up abruptly. "Gotta go."

And she was gone.

I didn't sleep much that night. In fact, I didn't sleep at all. Instead, I spent all night cooking for the party the next day. I made roast pork, black beans and rice. Typical Cuban fare and enough to feed the more than 200 people I hoped would turn up.

I'd sent invitations out to all my friends and customers telling them the store was re-opening, and asking them to come and party with me. The TV commercial had aired and I'd made enough food to feed a small army. I'd also ordered a couple of kegs of beer. I really hoped I wasn't going to run out. Pretty much everything was ready for the grand re-opening of Sergio's Jewelry Store.

The following morning dawned bright and clear. I sat out back and smoked a cigar as I watched the sun come up over the water. It was beautiful. I knew it was a good omen. It was going to be a good day.

I was right.

The day passed pretty much in a blur. From early in the morning, as soon as we opened, the turnout was amazing and much larger than I'd hoped for even in my wildest dreams. And, I can have some pretty wild dreams.

I started the day at the store. I wanted to personally greet everyone who came by and shake each of them by the hand. Everyone wanted to know about the robbery and I had to tell the story over and over again. So many times, in fact, that my voice started to go. It was a good job there was plenty of beer to drink or I might have lost the ability to speak altogether.

I'd decided to hold a grand re-opening prize draw as a way of thanking all the people who came out that day. Everyone who came to the store got a ticket for the draw and I'd chosen a number of stainless steel diamond and gold bracelets to give away as prizes. I'd made up my mind to give away quite a few of them because I wanted lots of people to have a chance of winning.

When it came time to draw the winning tickets, the store was crowded and so was the parking lot. It was like a July the fourth party. Everyone was eating and drinking and having a good time.

I was supposed to be drawing the winning tickets at Mick's bar, but I couldn't get across the mall because so many customers and well wishers wanted to stop and chat. The allotted time for the draw came and went, and I was still no nearer to Mick's place.

My friend Beth Painter and her wonderful husband Jim eventually had to come and rescue me.

"Sergio," Beth had to shout to make herself heard. "You'd better get over to Mick's place before there's a riot. People are waiting for you to draw those winning tickets."

The crowd in the pub made me feel like a million dollars when I did eventually get there. I was overcome with hellos and hugs and kisses. There must have been at least 200 hundred people there and I felt humbled and close to tears to know that so many of my friends and customers had shown up to support me.

I had to tell the story of the robbery again before I was able to draw the winning tickets and give the lucky winners their prizes. Then, I went back to the store and shook more hands and told the story a few more times as the day wore on.

The food all got eaten and the beer drunk. Mick helped out by bringing more food and drinks over for some of the guests. Most importantly, we sold a lot of jewelry.

When we'd closed the store and packed everything away, I finished the day as I'd started it, with a cigar.

If I'd sat down and mapped out the best-possible scenario for my re-opening beforehand, the day itself would have surpassed it. There was no doubt about it, I was back and so was my luck.

CHAPTER NINE

I didn't know what time it was when the phone woke me, but it was late. Or early. It was a few weeks after the re-opening and I'd been working long days in the store, drinking and playing poker with my Rough Rider buddies in the evenings and then falling into bed exhausted, only to get up and do it all over again. Good times.

I fumbled for my watch, trying and see what time it was, but only succeeded in knocking it to the floor.

I grabbed the phone. "Yeah." It came out more abruptly than I'd intended. I didn't like late-night phone calls. They usually meant only one thing— trouble.

"Sergio?" The voice was vaguely familiar, but I couldn't immediately place it. "Did I wake you?"

Talk about a stupid question. "Of course you damn well woke me. It's..." I was about to say what time it was, but realized I had no idea.

"Two-thirty," the voice cheerfully finished for me. "In the morning. This is your Uncle Frank, by the way."

Uncle Frank. Now I recognized the voice. My dad used to call his brother, my Uncle Frank, trouble because Uncle Frank was involved with the mob. When we moved to Florida, Uncle Frank continued working for the mob. He's retired now. I think.

I cleared my throat. "Frankie baby. Is everything OK?"

"Yeah, yeah, Sergio, everything's good. I heard about your bit of trouble though."

I'd managed to find the bedside light and flicked it on. I found my watch and checked the time. Uncle Frank hadn't been kidding, it was two-thirty.

"My bit of trouble?"

I heard him take a breath and then exhale. I figured he was smoking a cigar, probably Cuban, too, knowing Uncle Frank. He always liked the finer things in life.

"Your store, son, getting robbed like that. I would have called you sooner to talk only there wasn't much I could do about it then."

I was confused. "Well, it's nice of you to call, but I'm kind of getting back on my feet now. The store's open again and the cops have finally decided that I didn't have anything to do with the robbery."

"Still haven't found out who did it, though, have they." It wasn't a question.

I knew that tone of voice. I was paying full attention, all vestiges of sleep long since gone. "Do you know something about who robbed my place, Frankie?"

"If it was my place," he paused to suck on the cigar again. I heard the chink of ice in a glass and then he swallowed. "I'd damn well want to know who robbed me and I'd also damn well want to make sure they never did it again. That they couldn't ever do it again."

He chuckled. "Kind of hard to do fucking much of anything without hands."

I believed him. Frank was ruthless, but then you don't survive in the mob by being a nice guy.

"You want these guys, Serge?"

"Shit! Are you fucking kidding me? Of course I want them. I spent a lot of time and effort trying to find them until the cops told me to back off."

Another laugh, dismissive this time. "Fucking cops couldn't find a piece of shit up their ass if you sent 'em a map to the place."

I laughed. "You're right about that. Although one of the cops investigating the robbery is pretty fucking hot."

"Stop thinking with your dick, son. If you want the guys that ripped off your place you need to check out your store. Right away. I had my boys leave a little present there for you. I think it'll help you find the bastards. But, be quick, you don't want anyone else finding it. Trust me on that."

The phone went dead. That was Uncle Frank all over, he never said goodbye, just hung up or walked out. Interesting guy.

I jumped out of bed and pulled on my jeans and a shirt, wondering what the hell he might have left for me at the store. I jammed my .45 caliber 1911 Gold Cup semiautomatic into the waistband of my jeans. I'm comfortable with guns and rarely leave home without one, and I certainly wasn't about to head out without my trusty .45 that night.

I'd convinced my dad to buy me my first rifle, a .22 caliber Winchester semiautomatic, when I was 10 and my first 12-gauge shotgun when I was 11. I still own those and every other gun or rifle I've ever acquired. I only ever buy guns: I never sell them.

It didn't take me long to get to the store. There was no traffic and I drove fast. When Uncle Frank told you to get somewhere quick, it paid to get there real quick.

I drove into the parking lot and cruised slowly along to the store, pulling up at the curb in front of the entrance. There was something big and bulky leaning against the door. I grabbed a flashlight from the glove compartment and got out of the Hummer, leaving the engine running and the driver's door open just in case I needed to hightail it out of there fast.

Whatever was propped up against the door was encased in a black garbage bag, which was open at the top. I pulled down the plastic and found myself looking at the body of a man.

I stumbled backwards. "Fuck."

Then I realized the man was breathing. He was unconscious. His hands were duct taped together behind his back. More duct tape covered his mouth and blood from a wound on the side of his head smeared his face, but he was most definitely breathing.

So, this was the 'present' Uncle Frank had left for me. Nice. But what the fuck was I supposed to do with it? Turning the man over to the cops would only invite too many questions I couldn't answer. And maybe, just maybe, he could answer the question I wanted answering more than anything: who burglarized my store. After all, that was what Uncle Frank had said. Whatever I did, though, I was going to have to do it soon. Before someone saw me—and him.

I wrenched open the rear door of the Hummer and grabbed hold of the unconscious man. It took me a couple of minutes to get a good enough hold on him to be able to drag him to the Hummer. Unconscious people were damn heavy. Was this what it felt like to move a dead body?

Finally, I managed to manhandle him into the back of the truck. Thank God for all that weightlifting and running I'd been doing. I made sure the bag was away from his face so he could breathe and then I covered him with an old blanket. I didn't want anyone looking in the Hummer at some traffic lights or something, seeing a duct-taped body and calling 911.

When I started moving the man into my truck, I wasn't sure what I was going to do with him. By the time he was all neatly covered with the blanket, I knew. I jumped into the driver's seat, checked how much gas I had in the tank and headed out toward the highway.

Before long, I was driving north, out of Florida and into Alabama. The roads were quiet and I had a clear run to the State line. I slowed down when I got there. I didn't want to risk getting pulled over. I was glad, too, because a couple of miles into

Alabama, I saw a trooper sitting in his car, which was nearly obscured by the bushes.

As always, the Hummer ate up the miles. I glanced at my passenger a number of times, but he didn't move. If it hadn't been for the fact that his nostrils flared every time he breathed, it would have been tough to know he was alive. I wondered when he would wake up. I hoped it wouldn't be until I got to my place in the woods and had him tied up.

I filled up with gas at a station on the highway. I also picked up some food and coffee to keep me going—and keep me awake.

It was mid morning when I turned off the highway and bumped slowly down the dirt track to my hunting cabin. No thoughts of stopping off to see old Vickie Mae Walker this time though.

I pulled up in front of the cabin. It didn't look so bad in the early morning mist that foretold it was going to be another hot and humid day. I checked my passenger. Still out cold. Good. I didn't want him waking up just yet. I wondered what Uncle Frank's 'boys' had knocked him out with. It must have been more than just a blow to the head.

I jumped from the Hummer and stretched. I was tired and stiff from the drive, but also more wide awake and alert than I'd been for a long while. My heart was hammering in my chest and the adrenaline was pumping hard. I was excited.

Scared, too. A bit like my first hunt. The first time I'd killed a white tail. Exhilarating and a little frightening. And not for the squeamish. But, I'd found I didn't mind the blood. In fact, I'd found I actually quite liked it.

I pulled the man from the back of the Hummer. Getting him out was much easier than getting him in. I ripped off the plastic bag and threw it in the garbage. I knew I'd have to make sure I took everything away with me, just in case. I didn't want to leave any evidence behind.

It took me a while to string the guy up onto the rack I used for gutting deer. He was heavy. He felt heavier than any buck I'd killed, that was for sure. Eventually I had him tied up securely, arms above his head, which flopped against his chest.

By the time I finished, I was sweating and breathing heavily. And hungry. Before I ate though, I got out my razor-sharp skinning knives. I keep them at the cabin because it's the only place I ever use them and there's no point in bringing them back and forth all the time. I carried the flat square knife case back to the porch and laid it on the table in front of me. Then I dropped into the battered old rocking chair, ripped open one of the packs of sandwiches I'd bought at the gas station and popped open a beer.

I chewed on the sandwiches like a starving man, gulping them down in two or three mouthfuls. It was an interesting breakfast, but it tasted pretty damn good. I wiped the back of my fingers across my mouth to brush away the sandwich crumbs, cracked open another beer and mopped the sweat from my head with my hand.

I kept my knives in a black canvas case. I figured it for a moment before pulling the zipper open around all three sides. The case unfolded like a large flat book, but instead of pages on each side, there were neat rows of gleaming knives. All shapes and sizes. There was a skinning knife, a gut hook, a drop point, a clip point, a saw blade. All with rubberized pachmayr-type handles for good grip even in the slipperiest of conditions. And blood was pretty slippery.

These knives were my old friends and I remembered my first kill as I drew the six-inch Buck Special from its sheath. It was a perfectly balanced blade with a blood groove, satin-finished stainless steel that gleamed in the bright sunlight. Beautiful.

I love deer hunting. Pitting my wits against a deer's superior senses is a thrill unlike any other. What most people don't realize is that in the wild, deer have the advantage. They can see, smell and hear a hunter long before the hunter knows they're there.

I love checking the lay of the land for natural crossings and deer signs, and trying to find the best place to set up my stand. White tail deer tend to use the same crossings as their ancestors. If I can find a crossing with signs that deer are still using it, like droppings, rubs or scrapes, I know the chances are I've found a good place to hunt. Rubs are where a buck will rub his antlers against a tree and literally rub the bark off. scrapes are where a buck paws the ground leaving it bare.

Once I've found a good place to hunt, I have to sit and wait patiently, sometimes for hours without moving a muscle, for an unsuspecting deer to wander by. If a deer does wander past— and often I can sit for hours and see nothing—it has to be a buck with big enough antlers before I'll consider shooting it. Wounding an animal is unacceptable so I also have to have a perfect shot, one that ensures the deer will be dead before it hits the ground. Then, and only then, will I take the shot. And, when I shoot, I don't miss.

When I first started hunting, I joined a club. It was full of good ole boys, typical American rednecks. My first time out there, one of them asked if I was Italian or Cuban. When I told him I was Cubarican, he said, "Oh, so you're one of those, are you?"

It was clear they didn't like my ancestry, but they needed the dues and my money was good even if I wasn't. They weren't about to make it easy for me though. At least not to start with.

Soon after I joined the club, I got screwed by one of the other hunters. His name was Gerry and he was big, balding and red faced. He was always out of breath and always sweating.

I was new to the club and was trying hard not to do anything to upset anyone, but whenever I set up my stand, I'd get a call from one of the other hunters telling me it was in a place they'd staked out for themselves. So, I'd take my stand down and find somewhere else. Only for the same thing to happen again. They didn't think a 400 lb Cubarican from the Bronx could possibly know anything about hunting and probably thought they'd find it easy to make me give up and leave. But, like I always say, payback's a motherfucker and I decided was going to have fun teaching Gerry and my other new friends in the hunting club a thing or two.

It wasn't long before I got my chance. I knew the guys in the club thought you could only find deer in the middle of the forest so, to avoid any more calls from members saying I'd set up my stand in a place they'd already staked out, I went out to a wide-open cow pasture about a hundred acres big. In the middle of the pasture was a bottom, which was shaped like a soup bowl and had probably been caused by an ancient sink hole. I knew deer liked terrain changes so I crawled quietly to the rim and peered in, being careful not to silhouette myself against the open pasture. I was there for only a moment or two before I heard the sound of a deer walking on the dry leaves that carpeted the bottom. It was a big doe. And I knew that wherever there's a big doe, there would eventually also be a dominant buck. I'd found my natural crossing. I eased my way back away from the rim on my hands and knees so that I wouldn't spook the doe. It was time to get ready to hunt and the first thing I needed was a way to lure that buck.

The next morning, I took an old comforter that had belonged to my grandma, cut a hole in the center and put it on like a poncho. It was the colors of the land and I knew it would make great camouflage. I also figured it was appropriate as I always felt my ancestors were with me when I was hunting.

I went to a natural crossing I'd noticed a few days earlier. It had so many tracks, it looked like the Ho chi Minh trail. It was here I was going to set up an ambush for a doe. I wanted the doe for her tarsal glands, but I'd only shoot one whose glands were very dark, signifying she was in heat. The smell of a doe in heat is the best lure for a buck.

I wore rubber gloves and walked carefully to avoid stepping on the trail. I didn't want to risk spreading my scent around and scaring off the deer. To my left was a high hill and on my right was a clearing with a big tree stump in the middle of it. Stealthily, I made my way the 40 yards to the stump and sat down, covering myself with the comforter poncho and a camouflage headnet. And, there I sat and waited for deer to come down the Ho Chi Minh trail.

It wasn't long before I saw movement to my left. In hunting, you don't look for deer, you look for movement. Today, the flicker I saw was the ear of a big doe in thick cover. She was looking carefully my way, checking for possible danger before heading across the clearing. This morning, she saw nothing but a tree stump, and she slipped out of the woods, closely followed by two more does. The third was big and had black tarsal glands.

I brought my rifle to my shoulder so slowly it felt like it took forever. With both eyes open, I put the rifle's sight just behind her front shoulder and squeezed the trigger. When the noise of the 30/06 dissipated, the doe was lying dead on the trail and her friends were already in the next county.

I loaded the doe into the back of my truck and took off for the 80-mile round trip to Clay Williams' hunting camp. I wasn't about to skin her at my own camp and risk alerting the guys in my hunting club and having them figure out what I was up to.

Clay was a real Alabama hunter. He was my age, but had been born hunting and had forgotten more about it than I'll ever know. He behaved like a racist, which is something I can't stand, but with Clay it was just an act. I knew he went out of his way to share the venison from the deer he killed with some of the poorer Alabama blacks in his community. Clay had taught me just about everything I knew about hunting. His knowledge of nature and deer was like an outdoors encyclopedia, and I was eager to learn. He once told me that no one had ever asked him as many questions as I had.

I pulled up to Clay's camp and got out of my truck. "How you doing, boy?"

Clay grinned when he saw the doe. "So Sergio, did your sorry Spanish ass accidentally run over a deer with your truck? 'Cos I know you Yankee Tampa boys can't shoot worth a shit. Hell, when the deer see you in the woods, they don't run away. Nah, they laugh and say, 'It's just Sergio' and then go back to eating."

He walked around to the front of my truck and pretended he was looking for damage from where I'd supposedly hit the deer. Then he laughed and helped me get the doe onto the skinning rack. He disappeared and returned with a bottle of Wild Turkey 101, two shot glasses and two cold beers. It was only 9:30 in the morning, but it was our tradition to have a shot and a beer to celebrate our hunting good fortune.

Less than half an hour later, the doe was in the cooler resembling neatly-trimmed butcher meat. I'd eat the venison, use her hide and employ her prized tarsal glands to hunt a buck. By 12:30, we'd enjoyed three more shots and three more beers, and I reckoned it was time to take a nap before heading back.

In Alabama, it gets dark around 6:30 during hunting season and I'm usually in the woods by 3:00 pm at the latest for an evening hunt. Today, though, it was after four before I'd slept off the Wild Turkey and it was 5:30 when I got back to the rim of the bottom. I'd decided to hunt from the rim because I didn't want to risk spreading my scent by touching anything or walking through the bottom.

I hung the tarsal glands, which I'd cut up into eight pieces, in a line from the rim to a fallen tree I'd noticed on my first visit. The tree was where I was going sit and wait. I hung the glands so that the wind would blow the scent from behind me toward the way I was looking.

It wasn't long before I heard swishing sounds. I slowly raised my rifle and carefully scanned the area for movement. My heart jumped as a monster buck filled the scope. He was a 200 pound stud, about 175 yards away and crossing ground fast as he sniffed his way directly toward me and the tarsal glands behind my back. But I had no clear shot and I only take clear shots. I won't risk wounding an animal.

When he was 75 yards away from me, he suddenly raised his head and I knew he must have smelled me. He lifted his nose high in the air, then turned. Finally, I had my shot and I took it. I saw the buck rear up and heard a crash, but it was too dark to see where he had fallen. Or even if he had fallen.

I prayed that I'd not wounded him as I slid on my backside down the leafy hill. When I reached the bottom, it was pitch black. I couldn't see anything. My heart was beating hard as I searched. Then, I took a step backward and stumbled over his body. It had been a clean kill. I grabbed his antlers and started counting points. I could hardly believe it when I realized this monster was an 18" spread and a perfect 10 point.

I was happy as a pig in shit. I figured my kill would help me get accepted by my new hunting club. Was I ever wrong.

The very next time I went down to the bottom, I saw that Gerry had heard about my kill and set up his stand right by my tree. I called him up and told him that I'd staked out this place for myself. I asked him very politely if he'd move his stand. He refused. He said he'd done a lot of work down there and had even set up a corn feeder in the bottom. He was such a stupid idiot, he didn't even realize that in setting up the feeder, he'd spread his scent all over the place and ruined the whole area.

I was so pissed. I'm a pretty friendly guy, always ready to help someone in need, and I have a very long fuse, but when someone lights that fuse, there will be fireworks. I'd been polite when they'd told me to move from every place I'd set up before, but Gerry taking over the bottom like that was too much. He had no idea who he was dealing with. If someone messes with me or steals my stuff, I always get my revenge one way or another. And, I can be the most patient man in the world while I'm waiting to get it. Gerry was about to get a lesson he was never going to forget.

Before my next hunting trip, I collected two gallons of piss. By the time I went back up to the camp, it was pretty rank and smelly from sitting out in the sun. I took the piss out to the bottom and poured it over every deer sign I could find: scrapes, rubs, game trails, everything. I infected every place I figured a deer might walk with the smell of human pee. Then, I poured a quart of the stuff into the corn feeder Gerry had been using to attract deer. I still had about half a gallon left, so I walked up to his new stand and used a basting syringe to inject the urine into his cushion. Every time he sat down or moved, the cushion would give off a little puff of scent like a human pee air freshener. What was left of the urine, I poured into the hollow aluminum tubes that supported his stand. I made sure there was no way any buck or doe would ever come anywhere near this area again.

Then, I called Gerry up and told him I'd seen another monster buck feeding on his corn in the bottom. I wanted to make sure he only hunted in that spot. Old Gerry took a whole week off work to hunt that bottom, but came up empty. I didn't. The very next Saturday, luck smiled on me again and I killed a 189 pound 10 pt buck with a 20" spread.

When Gerry rolled into camp that evening, I called him over and said, "Gerry old buddy, look what I shot in our spot."

Gerry stared for a moment and then, without so much as a word, packed up his stuff, quit the club and went home, taking a little Sergio pee smell with him on his stand and cushion. Like I always say, karma's a bitch.

The combination of warm sun, cold beers and all-night drive was making me sleepy. I leaned back in my chair, propped my feet up on the table and closed my eyes against the morning sun. It was going to be a beautiful day.

I wasn't sure how long I dozed or what woke me, but when I opened my eyes I saw that the man on the skinning rack was awake. He was staring at me.

I stared back. The last buck I'd hung on that skinning rack had been that majestic and muscular 189 pound beauty. This guy, with his greasy ponytail and crack-head skinny frame, looked diminutive and pathetic by comparison. I almost felt sorry for him. Almost.

I grinned. I was going to enjoy this. "Oye Papito. It's time to have a party."

I cracked open a beer and drank slowly, as if I had all the time in the world. I walked around him and looked him over carefully as if searching for a soft spot to attack first. I saw the confusion in his eyes although his face remained immobile. He had no idea who I was or what I wanted and he was scared, but he was trying very hard not to let it show.

I sat back down and finished the beer, giving him time to stew and wonder what the fuck was going on. Finally, I stood up and stretched, grabbed my bottle of Wild Turkey 101 and crossed to the skinning rack. He struggled as I approached, but he was tied good and tight. I'd made sure of that. There was no way I wanted this guy getting away from me now. I pulled the duct tape from his mouth, yanking out plenty of facial hair at the same time and leaving patches of red and angry-looking skin behind. It must have hurt like hell, but he hid it well. I figured he fancied himself one tough dude. I'd taken on tough guys before.

"Who the fuck are you?" the guy's voice was hoarse and he had a heavy accent. Probably Cuban. "What the fuck do you want?"

I watched him struggle, trying to loosen the ropes tying him to the rack. "No point in struggling, my friend, I know how to tie a good knot. And you're going to need all your strength."

"I'm not your fucking friend."

He stopped struggling all the same. He probably realized I was right about the knots.

I grinned. "That's kind of sad, because I was hoping you and me might party, motherfucker."

I grabbed his ponytail, yanked his head back hard and upended the Wild Turkey into his mouth and nose, making sure he breathed some into his lungs. I returned to my seat and watched his eyes bulge as he coughed and retched. I wondered what hurt worse, the 101 proof booze going up his nose and into his lungs or coughing it back up again.

"Fuck man, you're no fun to party with."

I watched him struggle some more, trying in vain to free himself. Eventually, the heat must have gotten to him because he gave up.

"Listen, you got the wrong guy. I don't know who the hell you are or what you want, but I have friends and they're not going to be—"

"You robbed my store. Back in January. Sergio's Jewelry. In Tampa, Florida. Do you remember it?"

"I don't know nothing about no robbery. In Florida or anywhere else. Like I said, you got the wrong guy."

His face was blank, but I could see the fear in his eyes and knew he remembered. I hoped he couldn't see the same thing in mine. For all my bravado, I'd never been a sadist although I could happily beat the shit out of someone if they'd disrespected or hurt me or a member of my family.

I shook my head and lolled lazily back in my chair, reaching into the cooler and popping open another beer. "Now, my friend, that's a shame because we can do this the easy way or..."

I picked up one of the knives and fingered it then looked up at him. "The fun way. For me, anyway. Not sure that being skinned alive is gonna be much fun for you."

He tried to laugh. "Listen brother, you ain't gonna hurt me and we both know it. So how's about you let me go now and I'll make sure my friends don't come back and do more to you than rob your store."

I poured a shot of Wild Turkey and swallowed it straight down. "I'm not your fucking brother, man, and I'm not scared of your friends. In fact, I'd like 'em to come back."

I took another shot of the Wild Turkey. Then jumped to my feet and kicked him hard in the groin. He gasped and I filled his mouth and nose with more of the liquor. He tried to spit it out, but I grabbed his chin and held his nose until he had to swallow.

I took another shot of the Wild Turkey and watched as he retched and then threw up all over himself.

"Do you know what fire ants are?"

He swallowed. I could see that he did.

"Nasty little bastards, fire ants. When they bite you they inject this toxic venom. It's pretty painful, kind of like being burned by fire, which is how they got the name fire ants. I hear that if you get bit enough times the after-effects can be deadly to some people."

I realized I was starting to enjoy myself and was even beginning to wonder how he would sound when he screamed. The feeling scared me. My heart was beating fit to burst. I'd never felt like this before. "Fire ants are attracted by fluids, especially on hot days. Did you know that? All I have to do is gut you like a deer, leave your insides trailing on the ground and they'll be here in no time to eat you from the inside out."

His eyes were wide, his face pale. Droplets of sweat beaded his forehead and stained the armpits of his shirt. He started to struggle again. The ropes around his arms were starting to rub the skin raw.

"I'll make one hell of a lot of noise," he threatened.

I shoved my face close to his and screamed at the top of my lungs. "Go ahead, you motherfucker. There's no one here to hear you except for me and the coyotes... oh, and the fire ants, of course."

"Shit, shit, shit. Oh shit."

A stain spread across the front of his jeans. The guy had pissed himself. His knees buckled.

I leaned in close, but not too close. The smell of urine and vomit was pretty overpowering. "You and your buddies shouldn't have picked on a Cubarican from the Bronx, motherfucker, because no one—and I mean no one—rips me off and gets away with it. So, what do want? The fire ants or to talk to me?"

I picked up my gutting hook and circled around him a couple of times.

"Fuck you stink." I could see he was trembling too.

I stopped in front of him and lifted up my arm, bringing the gut hook down hard and fast toward his chest. I let it just nick his skin, then pulled it out and down sharply, slicing neatly and quickly through his shirt.

He screamed, thinking I'd opened him up, but when he looked down, he saw there was only a tiny bleeding scratch. He closed his eyes and leaned his head back. "Ok, OK, what do you want to know?"

"Your next job? Where and when?"

"They'll kill me if I tell you."

"And I'll fucking kill you if you don't. Tough choice, huh? Only difference is that they have to find you before they can kill you, but I have you all neatly tied up and ready to go."

I could see he knew he had no choice. It's amazing how the mind can work to scare a person.

He told me their next job was in two days' time at a jewelry store not far from mine. I got all the details. The time they were supposed to meet and where. The address of the store and when they planned to arrive there. Everything.

"You realize I can't just let you go, right?"

He lifted his head from his chest. His face glistened with sweat and blood. "Fuck man. I told you what you wanted to know. Please. Just let me go."

"If I let you go now you might go and warn your buddies. And I can't have that." I shook my head and fingered my blade. "Nope, I figure you're just going to have to stay here for a while. At least until after the job."

"I won't tell them anything. I swear."

I wasn't listening. "Will they miss you if you don't turn up?"

He shook his head. "They'll just think I'm drunk or with a woman or something. Happens all the time."

I walked slowly back to the porch and sank into the old chair, rocking gently. I had everything I needed. But what to do with this guy? I couldn't let him go and risk him letting the other members of his crew know what he'd told me. I wasn't going to kill him though. Whatever else I was, I wasn't a cold-blooded murderer. I'd just let him think I was.

I sat and rocked and thought for a while. I popped open another cold beer from the cooler and rocked and thought some more. The sun was high in the sky when I reached a decision. I went into the cabin and called Uncle Frank. I'd never asked Frank for a favor before and didn't relish asking one of him now, but there was no alternative. After all, what else was I going to do with the guy? I couldn't leave him here tied up to the skinning rack. I couldn't take him with me and I sure as hell couldn't let him go.

Frank picked up on the third ring.

"Frankie Baby?"

"Sergee," he sounded in a good mood. "How did you like your present?"

I grinned. "I liked it fine. Fucking thank you very much. But, I'm kind of done with it now."

"Got what you needed?"

"Yep."

"That's my Sergio. Always knew you took more after me than your old man."

"Do you think you might be able to take care of it until after the weekend for me?"

There was a long pause. Finally, "Why after the weekend?"

"After the weekend, it's no more use to me and you can let it go."

Another long pause. "Where is it?"

I told him.

"I can have someone there in around six hours. Will it be safe there until then?"

I nodded. "I'll wait here and make sure."

"You owe me, Sergio." And the phone went dead.

That was why I never asked a favor of Uncle Frank. He meant what he said about owing him. One day, I knew he'd call in the favor.

I shoved the phone into my pocket and grabbed a bottle of water from the cooler. I unscrewed the cap and took it to the figure drooping from the deer rack. I poured some over his head and then into his mouth.

"Someone's coming to take you somewhere and keep you safe for a few days. They'll let you go sometime after the weekend. After I've dealt with the rest of your friends."

"How do I know I can trust you?"

I shrugged and poured more water into his mouth. "You don't. But you also don't have a choice. Anyhow, if I was going to kill you, I'd have done it by now. I'm not gonna ruin my good karma by doing that, but if the guys that pick you up find out you were lying to me about the next job, you'll probably find yourself floating in on the high tide in four separate garbage bags. Those guys don't give a fuck about karma."

A little after six hours later, a black Cadillac bumped slowly down the lane and into the dusty yard in front of the cabin. Two men got out. Without a word, they crossed to the man tied to the skinning rack. One of them jabbed a hypodermic into his neck and he rapidly went limp. The two men quickly cut him free and carried him effortlessly to the car. They dumped him unceremoniously into the trunk and shut it before climbing back into the front seats and driving slowly away. Neither of them had spoken a single word or even acknowledged I was there. I might have been invisible for all the notice they took of me.

After they'd left, I collected every piece of garbage I could find into a big pile. I removed the rope and duct tape from the skinning rack and put it with the garbage. When I was satisfied that nothing remained to tie me to the man, I burned it all and spread the ashes in the woods. Then, I carefully cleaned my knives with Clorox, dried them and put them back into the case. Satisfied I'd removed every trace of evidence, I threw the cooler into the Hummer and headed back to Florida. I had a lot to do and not much time in which to do it.

CHAPTER TEN

The following day, I paid a visit to the jewelry store that was supposed to be next on the list for the crew that had ripped off my place. The store, which was called Jubilee Jewelers, was surprisingly similar to mine. Like my place, it was located at the end of a small strip mall and close to a major highway.

At the opposite end of the mall was a coffee shop. I parked in the shade of a big palm tree and sauntered across the parking lot toward the smell of freshly ground coffee beans. It was early, but the sun was already burning the back of my neck. I wiped the sweat from top of my head with my hand; it was going to be a scorcher of a day.

The café was cool and empty, apart from me. I ordered a coffee—black, no sugar—and sat in the window from where I had a good view across the parking lot down to the jewelry store. I picked up a copy of the Tampa Tribune from the pile of newspapers on the counter and stretched back in my chair as I pretended to read it. I idly turned the pages as I watched the cars entering and leaving the parking lot. After a while, I got up and ordered a second cup of coffee.

"Pretty quiet mall, huh?" I said to the large, middle-aged woman behind the counter.

She put down the book she was reading. "Afraid so. It's busier first thing in the morning, at lunchtime and at the end of the day. There are a few office buildings just around the corner and a lot of the people that work there come in for stuff."

I took the cup of coffee back to my seat by the window. By the time I'd finished it, not a single car remained in the parking lot that had been there when I'd first arrived. I was sure no one was watching the jewelry store—not yet, anyway.

I thanked the ample woman behind the counter and left, walking slowly by the shops in the mall, glancing into the windows as I passed. I didn't slow down when I reached Jubilee Jewelers, paying no more attention to it than I had to any of the other stores. Then, I walked back to my truck, climbed in and started the engine. I sat for a moment, waiting for the inside of the vehicle to get cool. If they robbed this place the same way they'd done mine, they'd put a look-out in a car somewhere in this mall. The look-out in that vehicle would certainly notice another car parked for any length of time. They might even check it out and if they saw someone inside, they'd probably hightail it out of there. And that was the last thing I wanted. I was going to have to find somewhere else from which to keep watch.

As I sat enjoying the cool breeze from the AC, a few people dressed in suits and business attire started to arrive at the coffee shop. They came mainly from the far end of the strip mall. Across the road, I could see what looked like industrial units and office buildings. That must have been what the woman had been talking about.

I put the Hummer in gear and drove across the road and into the parking lot on the other side. It was perfect. I could park there and be just about invisible to anyone in the mall across the road and yet I'd be able to see everything. I went home happy.

I really wanted to focus completely on my plans for Saturday night. I know from experience that the most successful hunts are those where you've done all the necessary preliminary ground work. Where you've checked and double checked all the possible outcomes, and are completely prepared for all eventualities. But, I'd promised to support an ice-cream social that the Rough Riders were organizing in collaboration with our sister krew, the Thieves of San Lorenzo. You've got to be careful with the Thieves of Lorenzo or those beautiful ladies will steal your heart.

At the social, we serve ice cream to the kids at the Shriners' Hospital and their parents, but for the first time I found myself wishing I didn't have to go. I just wanted to be able to focus on my plans for Saturday. But, there was no way I was ever going to let those kids and their parents down.

I always have fun serving the sick children ice cream, peanuts, sprinkles and chocolate sauce, and persuading them into second and third servings. Helping them, just for a moment, to forget their troubles and illnesses and pain. The smiles on their faces never fail to warm my heart and the reality of their problems always puts my own troubles into perspective and reminds me just how fortunate I am to have my health and my wonderful children.

That day, I made sure everyone was in the lunchroom and enjoying their ice cream before heading out into the hospital to check if any kids had stayed in their rooms. There's always a child or two somewhere who, for some reason, can't or won't go. This year was no different.

As I approached a room, I and heard a small child complaining that he "did not want to do it." He sounded very determined not to do "it" whatever it was. I went into the room and saw a beautiful little seven-year-old black boy. He was healthy and rambunctious looking, and was stubbornly refusing to put on his prosthetic legs. This little angel was a double amputee.

I put a huge grin on my face. "Dude, you better get those legs on 'cos I got all the free ice cream you can eat, but you gotta get yourself down to the lunchroom to get it."

I gave him some beads and was so happy to see a big smile crease his little face.

"Ice cream?" he yelled.

"You bet."

He put those legs on so fast and I accompanied him to the lunchroom where I gave him the biggest helping of ice cream and introduced him to the prettiest and sweetest of the Thieves of Lorenzo, Becky Teten. I knew from past experience that she'd steal his little heart like she'd once stolen minc.

My Hummer sticks out like a sore thumb, so on Friday afternoon, I got a nondescript rental car to use to drive back out to Jubilee Jewelers. I'd even shaved off my signature goatee to make sure no one recognized me. This was like any other hunting trip and I was ready for a long night, only this time it wasn't deer I was hunting, it was people. I had a cooler of water and other soft drinks in the back of the car, as well as plenty of food. I also had a pair of good binoculars and my 1911 semiautomatic. I turned the AC to maximum cold and pushed a CD into the player. Pink Floyd's "Shine on you Crazy Diamond" came blasting from the speakers. I grinned. Apt. What I was about to do was definitely more than a little crazy, but I wasn't going to turn this over to the cops and run the risk of them fucking things up.

It didn't take me long to get to the mall. I cruised slowly through the parking lot and drove past the jewelry store without stopping. It was possible that the robbers already had the place under surveillance and I wasn't about to do anything that might tip them off. I drove out of the mall, across the road and into the parking lot of the industrial units on the other side. I pulled into a parking space behind a few trees and turned off the engine. Then I adjusted the car seat back as far as it would go and settled in to wait. With the binoculars, I had a perfect view of Jubilee Jewelers and most of the parking lot, too.

For a while, I watched cars come and go. After about half an hour, I realized that none of the cars that had been in the lot when I'd first arrived were still there. Good. That meant the thieves weren't there watching, yet.

Around six, the parking lot started to empty. By seven thirty, there were no cars left. By nine, I was beginning to wonder if I'd been lied to and given the name of the wrong jewelry store. I figured that wasn't really likely though. The guy would hardly have had the name of another jewelry store on hand like that, would he? Anyway, he knew I'd be back for him if his crew didn't turn up tonight.

Of course, it was always possible that they'd called the whole thing off because the guy hadn't shown up.

By ten, I really needed the bathroom. I turned off the interior light so that it didn't come on when I opened the door and slid quietly from the car. The trees provided some shelter and I did what I needed to do before getting back into the car and gently pulling the door shut behind me.

I was just in time to see a beige Chrysler 300 cruise into the parking lot across the street. It circled the stores before reversing into a space from where it had an uninterrupted view of all the stores in the mall, including Jubilee Jewelers. The car's lights went dark, but no one got out. After a while, I saw a bright red glow from the interior. Whoever was in there was smoking a cigarette and maybe drinking skimmed milk.

I would have given anything for a smoke myself right about then, but I wasn't about to do anything that would give myself away. My heart was hammering in my ears. It was actually happening.

I picked up my binoculars and focused on the car, watching. My mouth was dry and I really wanted a drink, but didn't want to risk having to go to the bathroom again. I tried not to think about how thirsty I was.

An hour passed. And then another. And still the other car sat and waited. There was no sign of life except for the occasional red glow that betrayed a cigarette being smoked.

I didn't see the rest of the crew arrive. What I did see was a slight movement on the roof of the jewelry store. I probably would have missed it if I hadn't been straining my eyes to see. The movement was stealthy, hard to notice in the darkness, but it was there. And there was the occasional muted flash of light. I waited. The moment had to be right. Too soon and they'd be able to bolt too easily and they might get away. I needed to wait until they were working to cut open the safes. Once they were inside the store doing that, they'd be occupied for a good while and less likely to notice anything happening outside.

Before long, the movement on the roof ceased and I saw a brief flash of light from inside the store.

I picked up my cell phone and punched in a number. It rang for a long time. I started to worry that she might not be home. It hadn't occurred to me that she might not be there. It would really screw up my carefully laid plans if she wasn't.

Eventually. "Yeah?" Her voice was sleepy.

"Did I wake you?"

"Who is this?" She sounded more awake now.

"It's Sergio Pages."

"Jeeze. Now look here, Sergio—"

"No time to explain." I didn't let her finish. "I've found the crew that robbed my shop. They're in the middle of breaking into another jewelry store. Right now. You need to get here and do your cop thing."

"What? How do you know—"

"Listen Detective, get your fucking ass out of bed and get over here with back up right now or I'm going in there with my .45." I was getting pretty pissed. This was not the reaction I'd been expecting from her. "They're here and they're breaking in. Right now. Are you going to come and arrest them or do me and my .45 have to deal with them? I have six magazines of ammo, chicklette."

"Shit. OK. OK. Where the hell is this place?"

I told her.

"You'd better not be fucking with me, Sergio Pages."

"I'm not. Just remember that they have a look-out in the parking lot."

"And where are you?" I could hear she was moving now, talking as she got ready to leave.

"Parked across the street. In a parking lot alongside some office buildings and industrial units."

"Stay there." It was her attempt at an order, but we both knew who was in charge now.

I ended the call and sat back to wait.

I wasn't sure what the cops would do. I just hoped they wouldn't scream up to the place with lights flashing and sirens blazing, giving plenty of warning to the thieves. I figured Ward was smarter than that. That's why I'd called her. Or, at least, I told myself that was why I'd called her.

They dealt with the look-out first, surrounding the car with such silence and suddenness that even I didn't know they were there until they'd ripped open the doors and forced the two occupants out and onto the ground face down.

Then, all hell broke loose. I saw the light of the swat team's flashbang grenades before I heard the thunderous explosions. Only then did the marked cars come racing up with lights blazing and sirens screaming.

There was so much movement, it was hard to keep track of it all. I watched as the cops crashed into the store with weapons drawn. A little while later, they started to lead people out. One of them tried to run, and there was a brief eruption of shouting as a number of uniformed officers took off after a shadow that darted suddenly across the parking lot. He didn't get far.

Each person that was led from the store was put into a separate police car and driven off. I wasn't sure how many there were.

After a while, I saw someone detach themselves from the group of cops across the street and head toward my car. The figure walked under a streetlight and I saw it was Ward. I grinned. She looked happy.

She stood in front of my car for a moment, hands on hips, and then came and rapped her knuckles on the driver's window. I wound down the glass.

She leaned into the car, forearms on the top of the car door. "Mr. Pages."

"Detective Ward. Fancy seeing you here."

"How the hell did you know what was going on here tonight?"

I shrugged. "Let's just say a little bird told me."

"A little bird, huh? Did it sing?"

I grinned and nodded.

"You know, you should have told us right away when the little bird started singing. It could have been dangerous for you to be out here on your own."

"But it wasn't," I countered. "Besides, I didn't think you'd believe me."

She frowned. The furrow between her blond eyebrows and those big dimples in her cheeks just made her look cuter than ever. "You should have known that I'd believe you, Sergio."

"But Detective Gibson might not have and I couldn't take that risk. Anyhow, everything worked out OK. You got them all."

She nodded. "Yep, we got them all, including both the look-out guys."

She eyed me. "I guess I should thank you."

"How about having a drink or dinner with me instead?" That hadn't been what I'd been intending to say, but it had been what I'd been thinking. Actually, I'd been thinking about something a lot more intimate than a drink.

She leaned over and put her hand on my arm. Her fingers were warm, her skin soft against mine. Her fingers brushed the length of my forearm and down onto my hand. She squeezed it slightly.

"You're a really great guy, Sergio, and I like you a lot. I really do."

She tilted her head, her eyes dancing. "But someone like me needs a guy who wants to be with only me. And I get the feeling that you're not that kind of a guy."

I half smiled. "I could change?"

She grinned. "Yep, I'm sure you'd try. But, in the end, you are who you are. You like the ladies a little too much and sooner or later you'd have to kiss the pretty ones and I wouldn't like that. I wouldn't like that at all."

She removed her hand and shrugged. "It's kind of a shame, because I really do like you. But I have a feeling you're going to meet lots of pretty ladies who'll just love to go out with you. And who won't mind that you're not interested in only them."

She turned and started to walk away, then changed her mind and came back again. She pulled a pen and a card from her pocket. She scribbled something on the back of the card and handed it to me. "That's my home contact details. If you ever need my help, you just call me, OK?"

She leaned in close and lightly kissed the top of my head. "I mean it, Serge. We're friends, you and me. You did me a huge favor tonight and I won't forget it. Only don't you ever call me if you get pulled over for speeding or DUI or arrested for drunkenness. That would really piss me off."

She ran her finger over my clean-shaven chin. "Oh, and grow back the goatee. I prefer you with it."

This time she really did walk away. I turned the card over in my hand. She was one classy lady. And she was right about me, too. I really did like the ladies.

I drove home carefully, staying within the speed limit the whole way, much to the frustration of the cars behind me.

Damn but I felt good. That had been better than sex. Almost.

CHAPTER ELEVEN

If I thought things were going to get easier after I'd helped the cops catch the thieves who'd burglarized my store and cleared myself of suspicion in the process, I was wrong. Very wrong.

Although the cops arrested the entire crew that night, it turned out that they'd managed to lose the cigarette butts and milk carton that they'd collected from the parking lot at my store. They should have been placed in the evidence locker, but someone screwed up and they were gone. Without DNA from those or any other direct evidence, there was no way to categorically prove it was the same gang that robbed my store. The M.O. was the same though and the chance of it being a different crew was remote, but there was no direct proof and I'll probably never know for certain, although my gut tells me it was those guys.

The cops seemed satisfied though and the insurance company paid out in full, but I'd been badly underinsured and was left owing a lot of people a lot of money. I also still owed my ex-wife $500,000 and the American economy was tanking fast.

Retail sales in my store fell by 85 percent and the price of gold rose from $280 an ounce to $1,900, putting a price tag of $7,500 on a chain I might have sold for $1,000 back then. With people worried about putting food on their tables and clothes on their backs, they don't have money for luxuries anymore and they definitely don't have $7,500 to spend on a gold chain.

The other day a young woman came into my store. I've known her since she was a toddler, when she used to come into the place holding onto her mother's hand. Now, she has her own beautiful children, but she hadn't come to the store to buy anything. She was crying as she told me she was a single mom who'd lost her job a year before. She was about to lose her house and would have to live with her kids in her car. It was heartbreaking.

I wish the politicians in their ivory towers in Washington could have looked into that young woman's face. I did what I could to help, but our country is filled with far too many similar stories.

I had high hopes that President Obama would follow through with his promise to change the way things worked in Washington. But when he aligned himself with the likes of Nancy Polosi and Harry Read, he proved himself to be just as self-serving as George Bush and Dick Cheney and their Haliburton buddies were before him. Our politicians enjoy the kinds of benefits and retirement packages that most ordinary Americans can only dream about. If the leaders of our great nation truly care about our country, they should be taking a pay cut and giving up some of their benefits rather than voting themselves more. Politicians should be tightening their belts just like the rest of us are having to do.

That's why I mention politicians in the commercials I make for Sergio's Jewelry. I want people to put pressure on our elected leaders, to make them start collaborating and doing what they need to do to put our country back to work rather than acting out of self interest.

America's politicians seem to spend their time fighting among themselves and our great nation is going to the dogs—and real people are losing their livelihoods—as a result.

I know I'll survive and so will my store, but I'm sad for my fellow Americans, especially those raising their families. It's tough out there.

I still do what I can for my community and participate in Rough Rider events. Not that long ago, my Rough Rider buddies and I were at a free party the City of Tampa organizes each year for the kids. They'd made a big Plexiglas-fronted toy box for us to collect donations of teddy bears for our teddy-bear runs. During the festivities, a young couple came up with two huge bags of teddy bears. As she placed the bears in the toy box, the young woman started to tell me how she loves the Rough Riders. After a while, I noticed tears were streaming down her face. She reached into the bottom of the second bag and pulled out an enormous teddy bear. She told me that this was the teddy bear the Rough Riders had given her son on Christmas Eve of the previous year. She went on to say that her son had died the very next day and that they wanted some other needy child to have the bear. By this time, we were all crying. Once again, I was reminded just how fortunate I was to have my health and my family.

Rebecca Ward was right about there being plenty of women, too. I'm not sure I'm cut out for the single life though. I really like being one half of a perfect pair and I'm still hoping to meet the right lady to spend the rest of my life with. For now, though, I guess I'll just have to make the best of things the way they are.

I don't know what the future holds, but I do know that whatever curve balls life throws at me, I will survive. I have my health, my wonderful children and my faith in God. And, that's all that really matters.

ABOUT THE AUTHOR

Born in Bristol, Somerset, and raised in various places in the South West of England, Nikki studied computer science and worked in high tech before realizing that she loved writing prose much more than she liked writing code. She was first published by the *War of the Monster Trucks,* a soccer fanzine for supporters of Sheffield Wednesday football club.

In her early thirties, Nikki moved to Canada along with her three small children and began to establish herself as a freelance writer. She contributed to a variety of Canadian and European publications, including the award-winning *Cycle Canada,* and wrote everything from speeches for government ministers and senators to video scripts, websites, whitepapers and more for a variety of private- and public-sector clients. During this time, she also added a fourth child to her young family and authored a number of full-length works of detective fiction, one of which was published in 1999.

Now a senior writer and communications expert for a major Canadian Crown Corporation, Nikki continues to write fiction in her spare time and is happy to be a self-confessed word nerd.